The Deliberate Death of Dr. Dudley

Intuitive Investigations, Book Two

BECKI WILLIS

Editing by SJS Editorial Services
ISBN: 978-1-947686-29-8

CONTENTS

CONTENTS	i
1	1
2	8
3	17
4	29
5	41
6	54
7	67
8	85
9	96
10	100
11	110
12	124
13	137
14	151
15	165
16	179
17	188

18   199

19   210

20   221

21   232

22   240

FROM THE AUTHOR   252

ABOUT THE AUTHOR   254

1

Tilly Orbach had a secret.

She longed to tell her friends about it, but she knew some things were best kept to herself. This was one of those things. It wasn't exactly a matter of life and death, but it was close enough.

She and a dozen other women gathered at the Lime Creek Community Center, planning for the upcoming Spring Fling. The chill of winter quickly leaked from the Ozark hillside as warm sunshine took its place. To welcome the season of new growth and fresh starts, each year the community came together in celebration on the third Saturday of April.

Back in the day, the Spring Fling was a chance to visit with friends and neighbors after a long, hard winter. For homesteads furrowed deep within the woods or perched high on a mountainside, the families often spent the winter months as shut-ins. The spring celebration had been a time to barter winter vegetables and handmade crafts for fresh seed, new supplies, and all the latest gossip.

These days, the celebration was no less important.

Times had changed, but not the people. They still craved interaction with friends and neighbors. And they still thrived on any bit of gossip they came in contact with. It was practically their duty to share it with others.

The event gained its fifteen minutes of fame when one of their social media posts, thanks to Clara Peabody's granddaughter, caught the eye of a Springfield television station news anchor. The anchor posted her plans to attend and invited others to join her, making that year's Spring Fling their best turn-out ever. The trend continued for two glorious years but with each year that followed, enthusiasm waned.

The committee struggled to come up with fresh ideas and new events and had slowly settled into the tried-and-true rhythm of the familiar.

"We'll have the annual cake walk, of course." Lucille Gardner was this year's chairwoman of the planning committee. With the details already scribbled inside her notebook—in ink, no less—Tilly wondered why they even bothered with a meeting.

Someone raised their hand. "Can we bring a pie, instead?"

"Yes, Clara," Lucille said with a long-suffering sigh. "You can bring a pie."

"I'm bringing cookies," another woman said. "Everyone just raves over my walnut and raisin cookies." Paulette Weeks looked quite pleased with her announcement.

Beside Tilly, Emmaline Freely grunted beneath her breath. "They rave about how awful they are," she said from the side of her mouth. "Everybody knows she grows the wormiest black walnut trees in the county. No amount of molasses and sweet raisins can cover that kind of bitter."

Tilly bit back a laugh, but not for the reason Emmaline might think. Someone else recently commented that Emmaline, herself, baked a bitter-tasting strawberry pie, but Tilly wouldn't dare tell her that. Not only was Emmaline her closest friend, but the source of the revelation was part of her secret. Keeping her silence wasn't a matter of life and death, but it was close enough.

Lucille moved on to the next item. "Children's events? Tinadra, I asked you to take care of that for us. Can you give us an update?"

No one else remembered voting on the younger woman to be in charge, but it saved them the bother. Most members were out of touch with what kids fancied these days.

By the time Tinadra Becker laid out her plans to entertain children of all ages, the older members were in awe.

Justine Paul raised her hand. "My boys are skilled in ax throwing, but how can that be safe for young 'uns?"

Tilly's mind wandered while Tinadra patiently explained the child-proof event. She had more pressing things to do than sit here pretending to be engaged in tedious details. Other than a few tweaks here and there—ax-throwing, for instance—the Spring Fling was as predictable as a late-spring frost.

Producing a quality batch of wild honey was less predictable and far more important than bounce houses and an obstacle course, no matter how high the inflatable slide was.

She forced herself to listen as Tinadra summed up her report with a confident, "Don't worry. I have everything under control."

Lucille nodded and moved on with her agenda. "The beauty pageant is one of the highlights of the Spring Fling. I took the liberty of appointing Gaye Nell to that task. With her previous experience, she makes the perfect fit. I'm sure everyone agrees, right?"

Put on the spot, there was a low murmur among the group, but no one voiced an objection. As a previous Flower Blossom Queen with experience in pageants, she was the obvious choice. The truth didn't stop the 'It would've been nice to have been asked' mantra murmured among themselves.

The pretty blond-haired former queen stood. She paused for the briefest of moments, allowing everyone time to appreciate her slim silhouette and her newest outfit. The casual chic style bore designer labels.

"We're right on schedule," Gaye Nell Maulkey reported in a pleased tone. "I've secured the school auditorium for auditions. Tryouts will take place two weeks before the event, with the queen announced during the opening ceremony."

"There will be a parade, right? The contestants will ride on their own floats?" someone asked. She turned to the others and stated proudly, "My great-granddaughter entered for Lil' Bud. She's more excited about the parade than the pageant!"

"Of course," Gaye Nell said. Her eyes twinkled as she revealed, "I've come up with a fabulous design for the thrones! This year, I thought it would be nice to shine the spotlight on the top two contestants in each division."

Only Tilly could hear Emmaline's snort. "That's because she was always runner-up in all those other pageants her mama put her in. Always the bridesmaid, never the bride."

There was a brief discussion about floats and the parade route, but the ultimate decision was the same as always: if it ain't broke, don't fix it.

"Do we have the judges lined up?" Lucille asked.

"I have commitments from two, but we still need one more."

For once, the committee chairman asked for the group's opinion.

"What about Reverend Moss?" Emmaline suggested.

Gaye Nell shook her head. "He has two granddaughters in the competition."

"What about your husband, Tinadra?" someone asked.

"He's the school principal. I'm sure he feels that would show favoritism toward select students."

Paulette raised her hand. "I nominate Doctor Dudley."

A ruffle of snickers moved throughout the room.

Paulette's chin tilted upward. "What's so funny about that?" Her tone was snippy. "He's an educated man with a distinguished background. He has an eye for art and things of beauty. I think he would make an excellent choice."

Tilly couldn't see who was speaking, but someone behind her quipped, "He definitely appreciates women, that's for sure."

"What's that supposed to mean?" Nelly Novak bristled at the comment.

"I shouldn't say anything, but I happen to know he's been *friendly* with some of his female patients."

"And how do you know this?" Paulette demanded.

"I have my ways."

Tilly turned to see who was speaking. Judging from the smug look on her face, she guessed it was Raley Bumgartner. Raley was too young to appreciate Doc Dudley and the way he truly *listened* to his female patients. Most doctors brushed away health concerns when it came to women of a certain age. More times than she could count, Tilly came away from doctor visits feeling like a hypochondriac. They placated women of her age, rather than treated them. Doc Dudley was one of the few physicians who truly understood the concerns of mature women.

"Rumors," Justine sniffed. "He's a respected member of the community. I think he makes an excellent candidate for judge."

"I think most of us agree on that point," Lucille said. "All in favor of asking Doc Dudley to be a judge say 'aye.'"

The room sang out in chorus. Raley Bumgartner was the sole holdout.

"I'll be happy to ask him!" Paulette volunteered.

In Tilly's estimation, she sounded a bit too eager.

"No need," Justine said as she airily brushed the other woman's offer aside. "I have an appointment with him day after tomorrow. *I'll* ask him."

Lucille gently cleared her throat. "As the head of the committee, I feel I should be the one to extend the invitation. I'll contact him as soon as the meeting adjourns."

Her haughty announcement didn't sit well with many of the other women, but no one spoke out. Most people thought twice before crossing Lucille Gardner.

Tilly wasn't worried about Lucille. She had more serious matters to worry about.

She had to keep her secret safe.

It wasn't a matter of life and death, but it was close enough.

2

She didn't mean to be eavesdropping.

After a hectic morning, Willow Alexander treated herself to a leisurely lunch at a quaint little diner she happened across. She had requested a booth by the window so she could enjoy the view of a gorgeous mountainside and the valley below.

Now that spring was officially underway in the Ozarks, everything was awash in color. Trees proudly wore their newest leaves of green, while flowering plants and trees popped with shades of the season. Even the rocky knobs and jagged cliffs wore hints of color where the most determined seeds pushed through cracks and fault lines.

At this time of day, the lunch crowd was long gone, and it was too early for dinner. With only a few other patrons in sight, Willow soaked in the solitude.

She felt their presence before she heard them. It started with a tiny chill crawling its way up her spine. The air around her felt thinner. Her senses went on high alert, making her hypersensitive to her surroundings.

Willow tried ignoring it at first. She needed the peace of a beautiful hillside and the temporary pleasure of no cares. If she wanted something to worry her mind, she would think about the case she was currently working on. The case was the reason she craved a few moments of solitude.

Then, she heard them talking.

She had no idea who sat behind her. Even if she turned around, she couldn't see over the high-backed seats, but judging from the voices, she guessed two men occupied the booth. Even though they spoke in a low tone, she couldn't help but hear.

"I told you," one said to his companion. "Boss wants payment."

"And he'll get it," the other man assured him. His voice sounded older and more dignified. "I have no intention of shirking my duties, nor the money I owe. I simply need a few more days. Ten, at most."

"Not good enough."

"There's no need to be unreasonable here, Pyle. Surely, a few days won't make that much of a difference. There are still a few loose ends I must tie up on my end but have no fear. I assure you, I will pay my share within ten days."

The man called Pyle answered in a menacing voice. "You don't understand, old man. I'm not the one who should be afraid. Have you forgotten who you're dealing with?"

Willow could feel the threat from one table away. The chill became a prick. The air turned from thin to a sudden heaviness.

The older man seemed unruffled. "Not at all. I fully understand the consequences of not paying my debt.

But ten days isn't too much to ask, now is it?"

"That's not my decision to make. Boss told me to collect, and that's what I intend to do."

"And your dedication to the job is commendable," the older gentleman assured him. He slathered on the compliment like whipped butter on a hot biscuit. "But there's no call for threats. The fact is, I don't have the money at this time. All the threats in the world—even physical violence, should it come to that—won't produce a penny more than I currently have."

Silence followed. Willow assumed Pyle took the words into account while he weighed his choices. It sounded to her like options were limited.

In a voice that raked like gravel across bare skin, he growled, "You have one week and not a minute more."

"One week should suffice," his companion agreed.

"One week, old man. That's it."

"Shall we meet here?"

"Are you insane? You'd bring a hundred-thousand dollars in cash to a public diner?"

Hearing the exorbitant sum, Willow bit back a gasp. What kind of arrangement did those men have? And what sort of deal involved that much cash?

The answer was obvious. Something illegal, of course.

Without shame, Willow now listened quite deliberately.

"Where, then?" the older man asked.

"Are you familiar with Murder Rock?"

"Of course."

"If it was good enough for outlaws, it should be good enough for this."

"That's private land, you know."

"Are you worried about breaking the law?" Pyle scoffed. "It's a little late for that, don't you think?"

"I simply don't want to be caught by the landowner."

"Leave that problem to me. You worry about having the money there at two p.m. next Wednesday. Not one minute after. Do I make myself clear?"

"Absolutely. Two p.m. on the dot."

Willow heard shuffling from the next booth. She assumed Pyle pushed from his seat. "Don't make me regret the extension, old man. This is a one-time offer."

Still unruffled, the older gentleman replied affably, "Two p.m., one week from today."

With somewhat of a growl, Pyle stalked off. His footsteps echoed heavily on the checkered tile floor.

Willow dared not turn around. She waited until she heard the bell jingle above the diner's door before peeking. All she could see was the rear of a blue pickup. She wasn't as familiar with body styles as her daughter, but she thought it was an older model Chevrolet. She couldn't see the man inside, and she wasn't about to lean out of the booth to get a better look. His companion still sat behind her.

That created a new problem for her. What if he turned around? What if he belatedly noticed her there and correctly assumed she had overheard their conversation? These men were involved in something illegal. That made them dangerous. And now she could be in danger, too.

The best she could do was make no sound and hope the man didn't see her there. His friend was still in the parking lot, no doubt reporting to his boss. She couldn't afford to have either man notice her or get a glimpse of her face.

Her plan was foiled when the waitress approached. "Can I get you anything else, hon?" the woman asked.

Thinking fast, Willow pretended to take an earbud from her ear. "I'm sorry," she apologized. "I was caught up in a podcast. Did you say something?"

"Just checking on you. Would you like to hear about our pies? Or maybe our chocolate fudge sundae?"

Willow needed to linger at the table as long as possible. The ice cream would melt too quickly, but she could push the pie around on her plate in convincing fashion. It would appear she was savoring every bite.

"What kind of pie?" she asked with a smile.

"Coconut cream, apple, and blueberry. The cook just took a peach cobbler out of the oven, but it needs to cool a bit before serving."

"I'll wait!" Willow blurted out eagerly. Looking embarrassed over her enthusiasm, she stuttered, "It's, uh, it's my favorite. Can you bring coffee with it? Freshly brewed, if it's not too much to ask." That should buy her more time.

"It might be another ten minutes," the waitress warned.

"That's fine. That should give me time to finish listening to my podcast."

"In that case, it's peach cobbler and fresh coffee coming up." The woman wrote the order on her pad, finishing with a flourish.

"No rush." Though she pretended to go back to her podcast, Willow listened as the server stopped at the booth behind her.

"What about you? Can I bring you anything else, Doc?"

Doc? Was that a nickname or a professional title? Willow wondered.

"I don't suppose you have any cookies, do you?"

"Peanut butter or chocolate chip?"

"What about one of each?" Willow couldn't see it, but she swore she could hear the twinkle in the man's eyes.

Chuckling, the waitress said, "I think that can be arranged."

"I, too, would like some of that fresh coffee."

Willow frowned. He had overheard her conversation. It would be only natural for him to assume she had overheard his.

What if he didn't believe her earbud ruse?

To be on the safe side, Willow dug the real thing out of her purse and stuffed one into her ear. She went so far as to find an actual podcast she had been listening to last night and queued it to the spot she had left it.

There. 'Proof' she had been minding her own business and hadn't heard a thing.

Willow glanced back at the front window. Darn! The man demanding payment was gone and she hadn't gotten a good look at his truck. He must have left while she was busy trying to look preoccupied.

Mission accomplished, she muttered to herself.

A few minutes later, the waitress appeared again. She carried a tray with a plate of cookies and just one cup of coffee. She stopped briefly at Willow's table. "I figured you wanted your coffee with your cobbler. It should be ready soon."

She moved on to the next booth. "Here you go, Doc. Fresh coffee and two kinds of cookies." She winked and confided, "Cook gave you double."

"Ah, she does know my fondness for treats," the man chuckled. "Please extend my thanks."

"Will do. Can I getcha anything else?"

"I believe this is more than sufficient."

Willow bit back a smile. The man was definitely a charmer. If she hadn't overheard the earlier conversation with his colleague, she would go so far as to use the term genteel. A throwback to days when people spoke eloquently and with a flourish.

Much to her ex-husband's dismay, it was a talent Willow had never quite mastered. As the wife of a rising star in the world of investments, they often entertained clients, and those elusive portfolios Marcus was so determined to obtain. She tried being the perfect hostess, but she didn't have her mother's flair for small talk, nor her tact for remaining silent at crucial moments.

Little did she know how important that skill would become in her new career. Once Marcus threw their marriage of twenty-eight years away in favor of a younger, bubblier woman—Mandy was proficient in small talk, if nothing else—Willow embarked on a new career. As co-owner of *Intuitive Investigations,* Willow was smart enough to know her strengths and weaknesses. Her mother and daughter were better suited for the finer points of social interaction, while she preferred staying in the background. It was easier to dig up dirt that way.

Even as a little girl, Willow had always been curious. Her favorite question was 'why?' If the answer wasn't exciting enough, she made up her own version. Being an only child, her imagination was often Willow's best friend. Imagination and curiosity were the perfect recipe for being nosy, and being nosy was crucial for private investigators. That's where the dirt came in.

"Here you go, hon. Piping-hot peach cobbler and fresh coffee." The waitress delivered the dessert with a pleased smile.

"Thanks. It looks delicious."

Willow was surprised to realize she meant it. She wasn't a big dessert eater, but the sight of the cobbler was enough to make her mouth water. It didn't take her long to indulge in a bite.

"Ooh. Hot," she said aloud. She did that thing tapping her fingers against her lips that people did in situations like this. It made no sense—the fingers actually restricted air flow to the scorched tongue—but it was a common reaction.

She waved the next bite in the air before tasting it. As the flavors hit her tongue, she couldn't help the word that escaped on a sigh, "Delicious."

Her reactions to the hot cobbler hadn't gone unnoticed. Unabashed, the man from the adjacent booth turned so that he could crane his neck around to see her.

"Pardon me," he said congenially. "I don't mean to be rude. But I take it the cobbler is good?"

"It's to die for!" The words popped out before she had time to assess the man. For Willow, that was practically unheard of. That nosy nature of hers was always on the alert.

As she had guessed from his voice, the man looked to be in his late seventies or early eighties, but he was well-preserved. He was a charmer, all right. His smile was open and engaging. He wore his white beard and mustache neatly trimmed and his suit impeccably neat. Willow saw wisdom etched into the lines of this face, and his eyes sparkled with a sharp mind. No matter his age, the man was still quite attractive.

Her mind had trouble computing the handsome man in front of her with a man involved in one-hundred-thousand-dollars' worth of illegal activity.

Hearing her uncensored reply, the man chuckled. "I'm glad to hear that. I've ordered a cobbler to take home."

"Excellent decision." Willow smiled her approval.

"Erma is a fine cook," the man assured her. "Living alone as I do, I enjoy a home-cooked meal as often as possible. I often have her cook some of my meals for me."

It was an odd statement to make. Having other people cook for you was the cornerstone of eating in a restaurant.

Maybe he wasn't as sharp as she originally thought...

3

Willow pulled into the parking lot behind *Intuitive Investigations*. She still marveled at how well her new SUV handled turns. Not to speak ill of the dead, but it was nothing like her faithful old Corolla. It had responded best to a good, hearty yank. This new car practically turned with one finger on the wheel.

Not so long ago, someone had blown up her old car, therefore forcing Willow to upgrade her ride. She couldn't dare admit such to her mother, but Willow absolutely loved the sporty little model she called Zipper. After the way she had ridiculed Ireland's sleek red Mercedes convertible, Willow refused to give her mother the satisfaction of saying 'I told you so.'

Willow punched in the code for the back door and entered the old brick building. At least she had gotten something useful out of her divorce, even if it wasn't the nice, three-bedroom home she had so lovingly decorated and cared for throughout their marriage. With a lot of hard work and determination, the unsightly downtown building was slowly turning into a showpiece. Willow's spacious apartment was right above their office, so the commute to work was easy enough.

She found Everleigh and Laura Beth singing along to a song on the radio, oblivious to Willow's arrival.

Good thing I'm not a client, she grunted to herself.

Laura Beth broke off mid-chorus when she saw her in the doorway. "Grammy!" A freshly turned twelve-year-old, Laura Beth was still young enough to fly into her grandmother's arms and give her a big hug.

"How was your day at school, Sweet Pea?"

"I made a 102 on my math test!" the preteen announced proudly.

"That's fantastic, sweetheart. I'm so proud of you."

"Back in my school days," Ireland Garrett pointed out, "there was no such thing. A+ was the best we could do. By the time your grandmother came along, they used numbers, but they only went as high as 100."

With a mischievous smile, Everleigh couldn't resist teasing her elders while bragging about her daughter's good grades. "Well, I guess kids are just smarter these days." She tossed her red curls for an extra bit of sass.

Willow wrinkled her nose and returned the sassy attitude. "Too bad it skipped a generation." She squeezed Everleigh's chin and brushed a kiss on her cheek to let her daughter know she was teasing.

"Sweet Pea, do you think you could make me one of your special coffees? The one with just a touch of caramel syrup?"

The girl nodded with enthusiasm. She loved using

the fancy coffee maker almost as much as her mother did. "I'll grind you some fresh beans, too!" she promised as she dashed off to the conference room's coffee bar.

Seeing the way Willow sank into her chair, Everleigh guessed, "Rough day?"

"And then some," she answered wearily. "I don't need the sugar, but the caffeine will be much appreciated."

"I'm sorry we had to throw you into the lion's den by yourself. What happened with the Fowlers?" Ireland asked.

As equal partners in the investigation firm, the three women were all licensed private investigators. The grandmother/mother/daughter team approached every case as a unit, knowing they each had their own strengths and weaknesses when it came to gathering information and solving crimes.

"I got what I believe is technically known as the run around." Her face scrunched with a scowl. "You couldn't get a straight answer out of that family if you used a squeeze press!"

"They're rather slippery, aren't they?" Ireland sighed in agreement.

"I know they have a bad reputation. They're doing something illegal. We know it, they know it, the entire community knows it. Yet they claim they're the victims here. They want us to find the person who they claim is stealing from them, but they're being very secretive about their business practices."

"I think it comes from years of dodging the law," Ireland said. "Denial comes second nature to them."

"Flat-out lying is more like it," Willow huffed.

Everleigh offered her thoughts on the matter. "Don't you imagine they're afraid to admit the truth to us, in fear we'll turn them in?"

"We're not bound by lawyer-client confidentiality, but we do have a duty to our clients. Unless they're causing someone direct bodily harm, or we witness them committing a terrible crime, we aren't required to report our findings or suspicions to the law. I've told them all this. They can speak to us in confidence."

"Sure, you told them that. But we're probably not the only people who say things like that and then double-cross them the first chance they get."

Her daughter had a point. "I guess so," Willow admitted. "But why hire us, if they won't *talk* to us? We'll be running around in circles."

"At least we'll be paid to ride the merry-go-round, dear," Ireland pointed out. "Why look a gift horse in the mouth?"

"Because this is the Fowler family we're talking about. I foolishly accepted this case over the phone"—she groaned at her own stupidity— "something we never do. But it's hard to say no to this bunch. They rarely ask for outside help, and they might see it as a rebuff if we turned them down. They have a reputation for retaliation, you know."

"Okay, so what do we know so far? What did you find out when you went to talk with them?" Everleigh asked. She perched on the edge of her desk, crossing her arms matter-of-factly across her chest and allowing a high-heeled sandal to dangle from one foot. Everleigh had a penchant for expensive, less-than-practical shoes.

"You want me to repeat *all* of it?" her mother clarified.

"Sure."

"Okay but brace yourself for the onslaught." Willow took a folder from her brief case and consulted the files within. "Claudette Fowler insists that someone is stealing from the family business of 'farming.'" She used her fingers to create air quotes. "She claims that she doesn't know who or how, just that it's happening. She's clearly the authoritarian in their family. If she says it's raining outside, her grown children ignore the sunny skies and pull out their rubber boots and umbrellas. So, naturally, they are emphatic about someone robbing them of their birthright. Mama Fowler seems to have put her faith in us, so by-golly, that's good enough for her kids, her grandkids, and her great- great-grandkids." She swung her arm with a punch of gusto. "The woman has to be old as dirt."

"Watch it," Ireland threatened quietly. "She's older than I am, but we actually attended school together. True, she did repeat more than one grade—and more than one time—but there's less than ten years between us."

Not everyone was as well-preserved as Ireland Perkins Garrett, but there was still a stark difference between the two old schoolmates.

"It looks more like thirty," Willow muttered uncharitably.

"She's had a hard life."

Willow cut the Fowler woman no slack. "Her lifestyle makes it that way."

"One thing I can say about Claudette is that she's

no quitter. She earned her diploma no matter how long it took. Don't assume she's stupid. She learns her lessons from life, and she learns them well."

Everleigh broke in to remind her mother, "You were telling me what you learned today."

"And I did."

"That's *it*? That's all you learned?"

"No, I learned some colorful new language today, as well. And that someone's wife was cheating with another man, but I lost track of who's who after about the first three or four sons. There're cousins and nieces and nephews living among them, and all of them know just one volume—loud. My ears are still ringing."

"You were gone most of that day. That's *all* you learned?" Everleigh repeated the question in disbelief.

"No, I also learned there's a diner in Gander that serves a delicious peach cobbler."

"And that took all day? We were here transcribing the Whitman case, you know." Suspicion pulled Everleigh's face into a frown. "Or was that what took you so long?"

"Believe me, I would have much rather have been here with you than with the Fowlers." She massaged her temples, which still throbbed with a dull headache. "By the way, do you happen to have any Celtic salt with you? I met a man at the diner who reminded me it should help. I keep forgetting to buy more."

"You met a man, huh?" Her daughter couldn't miss a chance to tease her. Actually, it was more like harassing her, despite the fact that she, too, was single.

Willow rolled her eyes. "He was closer to Landee's age than mine." Everleigh had given Ireland the nickname when she was learning to talk and, somehow, it had stuck.

"Silver-haired fox, or wrinkled old prune?"

"Closer to the silver-haired fox. And he's a doctor, so hopefully he knows what he's talking about." Her brows puckered. "Actually, maybe I shouldn't take medical advice from him. I have no idea if he's a general physician, a veterinarian, a dentist, or what. The name 'Doc' could even be a nickname, for all I know."

Ireland brought her a small jar. "He's right about the Celtic salt. That's why I keep some in my desk."

Twisting off the lid, Willow took a small pinch and put it on her tongue. The salty whang brought a slight wince to her face. "I may need some water before Laura Beth gets back with my coffee," she said with a cough.

"Here you go." Ireland offered a bottle of water. "No matter what kind of doctor he may or may not be, he's a smart man. The salt hydrates your cells and helps to balance electrolytes."

"Apparently, he's not too smart," Willow muttered. "He owes someone a hundred-thousand dollars, and they aren't happy about the fact that he can't pay."

Laura Beth returned with a steaming cup of coffee, topped by a fancy swirl of cream. Like her mother, the girl was on her way to becoming a first-rate barista. "Here you go, Grammy."

Willow eagerly accepted the drink. "You're a

lifesaver, Sweet Pea."

"Anytime." Dancing her way out of the room to the beat of the music, she disappeared.

With an affectionate shake of her head, Everleigh sighed. "That girl." In the next breath, she returned to the interrupted conversation. "A hundred-thousand, you say? If he is a doctor, his practice must not be doing so well."

In a sympathetic voice, Ireland wanted to know, "Was it the bank? Were they there to repossess something?"

"His blood, maybe. I'm pretty sure it wasn't the bank. He has exactly one week to pay. And get this. He's to meet the man and pay up at Murder Rocks."

"Murder Rocks?" Everleigh squeaked. "The ones Alfie Bolin used as a hideout for his outlaw gang back in the day?"

"The one and only."

"No, definitely not the bank," Ireland agreed. Her look turned to one of worry. "And they saw you? They know you were listening?"

"I hope not. The booths had high backs, and I pretended to have my earbuds in." She explained her ruse and how she lingered at her booth to avoid them.

"It doesn't sound like you succeeded." Everleigh frowned. "Not if you and this Doc carried on a conversation."

"At least the first man—the one named Pyle who was threatening him—didn't see me. I hid my face so he wouldn't see it, which means I didn't see his, either."

"Did you see him drive off? Did you get his license

plate number? I could trace it." The youngest of their three-women team was a whiz on the computer.

"Missed that, too. I was so busy looking preoccupied, I actually was. All I know is that he was driving a dark-blue pickup. I'm not the expert on cars that you are, but I think it may have been an older-model Chevy."

Everleigh thought for a moment. "They were meeting in Arkansas, but the drop point is in Missouri. If you at least saw the color of the plate, I'd know which state to look in."

"Sorry, I didn't get that, either," she apologized. "But come to think of it, don't you think that's a bit odd? Gander and Murder Rocks aren't even in the same state."

Everleigh shrugged. "Maybe this Doc is from Missouri, so meeting at a diner where people don't know him makes sense. Unlike us, the doctor probably isn't licensed to practice in both states, but Gander isn't far over the state line. Easy enough drive, without running into patients. How did you come about talking with this Doc person, anyway?"

"Pyle stayed in the parking lot, talking on his phone for several minutes. I had to stall so I ordered dessert. Unfortunately, so did the man the waitress called Doc. He turned around to ask if the cobbler was good, and we exchanged small talk for a minute or two. Neither of us introduced ourselves." With a shrug, she explained, "It wasn't that deep of a conversation."

"I don't suppose you got a look at *his* license plate?" Everleigh asked in a hopeful voice.

"I tried waiting him out, but the waitress came up

and they started talking. I took my chance to get out while he was involved in a friendly conversation. Hopefully, he's not the suspicious type."

"That could have been dangerous, you know." Ireland still wasn't pleased with the potential ramifications of eavesdropping.

"It's not like I was *trying* to hear them," Willow defended herself. "Not at first, anyway. Then I heard this Pyle saying the boss wouldn't be happy, and I could feel the threat in his voice from where I sat. The mention of a hundred-thousand dollars definitely caught my attention."

"We don't need to get distracted," Everleigh reminded the others. "We have enough on our plate with the Fowler family."

"Again, I'm sorry I got us into this mess. But we took the Whitman case pro bono, charging only for basic expenses. And the case before Whitman reneged on the final payment. I don't know about you, but I, for one, like to eat. Electricity is nice, too." Willow blew out a breath and took another sip of her coffee. "I felt we didn't have a choice about taking on this case, no matter how maddening it is, but now I'm regretting my hasty decision."

"Then let's get it over with as quickly as possible. We can collect our money and get out of Dodge," Everleigh said. "What's our next move?"

"Besides convincing Mama Fowler to open up and be candid with us? I have no clue. How do we find proof when we don't know what we're looking for?"

"I talked to my old friend Bertha yesterday," Ireland said. "She's a distant cousin, you know. I mentioned our current predicament, and did you know the Fowlers have kin in Texas? They live right there in The Sisters, and Bertha says they're known for being nothing but trouble. Two of the brothers are in prison on drug charges."

"They must have some sort of family franchise," Willow mumbled.

"And they told you *nothing* while you were there?" Astonishment still lingered in Everleigh's tone. It was hard to believe it took hours to learn so little.

"Nothing. All they said was that they were losing some of their harvest, and it cut into their profits. They want us to find out how and who is doing it."

"We knew that much when you took the job."

"Yes, and we assumed they would give us more information after that. Which was the point of today's visit." Willow set her cup down so she could rub her temples again. "Turns out, we were wrong about them volunteering anything else."

"I vote we give them their money back and find another case," Everleigh suggested.

"Can't."

"Why not?"

Ireland reminded her granddaughter why that wasn't an option. "Like your mom said, they rarely ask for outside help. In a strange sort of way, we should be flattered they came to us. If we backed out now, they might think we're double-crossing them. They wouldn't take that sort of disrespect lightly."

"And secondly," Willow added, "we can't afford to return the deposit. We'll need it to tide us over until our next case."

"I should have gone." Ireland realized her error now. "I could have persuaded them to talk."

"I'm not sure even your special touch could help in this circumstance."

"It would have been worth a try. Especially since I share a vague history with Claudette."

"As it is, I have a stakeout set for tonight, but we need all the information we can get. I don't need a special gift to know this case doesn't look promising."

4

Vern Dudley carefully navigated the stairs leading to his basement. At his age, he couldn't afford a misstep. With every year marked by the turn of a calendar, bones tended to deteriorate. If he were to break one now, it would take forever to heal.

His forever, at any rate. Vern was known as a risk taker, but not when it came to matters of health.

Once on solid ground, he felt more confident. No need to shuffle his feet or take tentative steps. Down here, he could move freely about in the wide expanse of his lab.

Vern whistled a tune as he turned on an additional set of lights. Without them, the space felt drab and depressing. Shadows lingered in the corners, and a clammy chill hovered along the concrete floor. The chill had a way of traveling through the soles of his shoes and up his legs. He found that a burst of bright lighting made all the difference. No more shadows. Even the floor seemed to warm beneath the glow of a thousand watts.

The drying room, of course, was a different

matter. It was important to keep the area dark to avoid degrading the product. He had a special corner for that, curtained off to keep the warmth in and the light out. Humidity and proper air flow was always a challenge down here, but he had finally mastered the process. With the proper heaters, fans, and drying racks, he could dry small batches in a relatively short period.

As always, the first thing the doctor did was consult the chart on his wall. He wasn't scheduled to turn the product until tomorrow, so he knew better than to disturb the process today. He could go straight to work at his table.

Vern pulled an apron over his neck, pulled the adjustable light down for optimal lighting, and placed the goggles snuggly over his eyeglasses.

Today, he was making tinctures. He was working with a small batch, so he didn't need to pull out the blender or any of his larger apparatuses. The Ninja chopper would do just fine. Vern was ready to start when his security camera beeped. Someone was at his back door.

He would ignore them. Inventory was low at the clinic, and he needed to get at least one batch finished tonight. His unexpected guest could wait.

Curiosity made him glance at the screen. Even though she wore a floppy hat and a scarf pulled around the lower half of her face, Vern recognized the woman on his back step. Lucille Gardner had terrible timing.

Should he ignore her and go on with his work? He hadn't actually gotten started yet. He could leave everything as it was and return when she was gone.

With any luck, she wouldn't stay long.

Noticing the pie plate she held in her hands, he decided the polite thing to do was greet his caller and invite her in for a visit. He pressed the intercom and spoke through the speaker. "Coming, my dear. Just finishing up on a few notes. I'll be right there." He removed the apron and goggles, turned off the brighter set of lights, and retraced his steps up the stairs.

Careful to lock the door behind him, he slicked his hair down on the way to greet her. A charming smile was in place as he swung the door inward. "I'm sorry to keep you waiting, Lucille. Please, come right in."

"I'm sorry to drop in unannounced like this." She was long past being a schoolgirl, but Lucille blushed like a teenager dropping in on her first big crush.

"Don't be silly. You're always welcome here." He made certain she was well inside the kitchen before brushing a kiss on her cheek. "Let's get you out of all that fluffery, shall we?"

"You'd better take this first." She handed him the pie plate before unwinding the scarf around her neck.

With both it and the hat tucked away on the small table beside the door, she turned back to her host. "I brought you a blackberry pie. It's from last year's berries that Paulette gave me. She had them in her freezer, but they should taste fine."

"Everything you make tastes more than fine, Lucille. Would you care to join me in the parlor?"

Lucille liked the way he called it a parlor. Just the way a proper gentleman would do. She offered him a coy smile. "I do like the way your sofa sits."

"Allow me, madame." He offered her his arm,

inciting more giggles as he escorted her into the other room.

"I hope I didn't disturb you."

"No, no, not at all," he assured her as he helped her sit. "I was just finishing up on a few notes from the clinic."

"You work too hard, Vern," she chided gently. "You really shouldn't bring your work home with you. You deserve to sit down and relax at the end of a long day."

"I'm afraid doctors can't always adhere to schedules, my dear. Emergencies and whatnot, you know."

"You had an emergency? I hope it wasn't too serious!"

"It wasn't a true emergency, but it did require immediate attention. I had to leave the office early, so I brought some of my paperwork home with me." He tapped the side of his temple with one finger. "I can't keep it all up here, you know. Keeping meticulous records are the cornerstone of a competent doctor and any legitimate practice."

"That's certainly you, Vern. You're the best doctor I know." She patted him affectionately on the knee. She had chosen the sofa so he could sit beside her.

"Thank you, Lucille, for the vote of confidence." She giggled again when he covered her hand with his and allowed it to remain there.

"I have a confession to make. I didn't come by just to deliver a pie."

"You didn't?" A smile hovered on his lips as he moved closer to her side. Releasing her hand, he draped his arm around her shoulders. "Why did you come, Lucille?"

When he nuzzled her neck that way, it was difficult for her to remember the real reason she had come. The *other* reason.

"Oh, um, I came to ask a favor."

"Anything for you, my love."

She swallowed hard. The endearment muddled her mind and turned her insides to a bowl of quivering jelly. "I—I seem to have forgotten..." At his chuckle, she recalled the second-most important reason for her visit. "Oh, yes. Yes, I wanted to ask you... that is, on behalf of the Spring Fling Planning Committee, we would like to invite you to be a judge for our annual Flower Blossom pageant."

He pulled away just far enough to look properly surprised. She didn't know that two other members had already contacted him with the same request. "Why, I'd be honored."

"You have such an eye for beauty and refinement."

He pulled her close again and whispered against her ear, "Why, yes, I most certainly do. I appreciate beautiful women such as yourself, Lucille."

"B—Beautiful?" She hadn't been called beautiful since her husband died. If she were being brutally honest, it had been a good forty years before that. Back when there was a hint of sparkle in her eyes and a bounce in her step.

"Yes, Lucille. You are a very beautiful woman." He touched her cheek with his hand, ignoring the wrinkles that pooled in his palm. "As you said, I have an eye for these things."

He kissed her until she was breathless. For once, she didn't care that her hair would get mussed or that her lipstick might be smeared. She was perfectly content snuggling with him on the couch, her head upon his shoulder as he showered her with compliments and kisses.

As his kisses grew bolder, Lucille stirred from her position. To her horror, she had somehow sunk further into the cushions, almost in a reclining position.

"Oh!" she cried. "Oh, my!" With her face ablaze, she struggled to sit up. To her further humiliation, the doctor had to give her a hand.

"You must forgive me, Lucille. I never meant to make you feel uncomfortable."

"I—I really must go!" She tried pushing herself to her feet, but her legs were as liquid as her insides.

"Please. Allow me." He was on his feet, offering her his hand.

Lucille wished she were brave enough to take his hand and pull him back down to the sofa to continue what they had started. But she wasn't that kind of woman.

She truly *wasn't*, she reprimanded herself sharply.

"Please, Lucille. Don't rush off. I promise I'll be a gentleman."

"I... No, I really must go.," she insisted. If she lingered any longer, she might discover she was exactly that kind of a woman.

He followed her to the kitchen, where she was hastily wrapping up in her scarf. She plopped the hat over her rumpled hair and reached for the door handle.

"Forgive me, my dear? I didn't mean to get so carried away. It's just that your beauty..." He dropped his head and shook it in shame. "I do hope you accept my sincere apology."

"There's—there's nothing to apologize for. I'm sorry I disturbed your work." She slipped quickly out the door and practically ran down the paved pathway.

"Thank you for the pie!" he called to her retreating back.

Vern blew out a deep breath as he shut the door. Her rush out the door was frustrating, but it hardly equaled that of yesterday's encounter with Pyle. Boss was being unreasonable. How could the man expect him to come up with that kind of cash in one week's time? Vern had suggested ten days, knowing that, too, was impossible. He was having trouble with cash flow these days. Production time was down, his lucky streak at the tables had dried up, and now, his supplier was giving him a hard time. With just twenty-four hours in one day, a man could only do so much.

When his phone rang, Vern jerked it to his ear without looking at the caller's name. The minute he heard Catherine's voice, he wished he hadn't been so rash.

"Father? Are you there?" Her high-pitched voice grated on his nerves.

He considered hanging up. He could always blame it on a bad connection. But she was his only daughter, and she was nothing if not persistent. She would keep calling until he answered.

She was doing the same thing with her same tired request, thinking that sooner or later, she would wear him down. Little did she know he was in worse financial condition than she was.

"Yes, Catherine, I'm here. How are you this evening, my dear?" He may be disgruntled, but there was no reason to be unpleasant.

"Fair, enough, I suppose. Considering."

He ignored the bait. "And the children. How are they?"

"How should I know? James is off in Hawaii with his surf board and the girl of the month. Who has time to call the woman who spent seventeen hours in labor to give birth to him? Maggie is busy with her own children and her career; I'm lucky if I hear from her three times a year. Nelson calls like clockwork on Mother's Day and holidays." She didn't mention it was the only phone privilege he had in prison. "If they weren't okay, I'd be the last to know. At least I still have Waylon."

If Catherine complained to her children the same way she complained to her father, he knew why they never called home. Waylon was the son who was too lazy to get a job and move out on his own. At thirty-something, he still mooched off his parents.

The same way his mother does you, Vern reminded himself darkly.

"And Winston?" he asked politely. He couldn't care less about how his son-in-law was doing but not asking would be rude. Vern prided himself on never being rude.

"The poor dear. His sciatica is still giving him fits. He had a job interview this morning but had to cancel at the last minute. The poor man couldn't even get out of bed."

Probably too hungover, if his guess was right. He

supposed even fast food restaurants liked interviewing potential employees when they were sober.

"Did he see the specialist I recommended?" Vern asked.

"Actually, that's one of the reasons I'm calling. We lost our health insurance last month, and we can't afford a specialist right now. We need to borrow a little more money, Dad."

Funny, how her formal greeting of 'Father' had suddenly turned to the softer term of 'Dad.'

"Catherine—"

"I know what you're going to say. You've already been so generous. I know Mom wanted me to have the money, but you're right to keep control while you're still alive. It only makes sense. But I just need a little. Enough to get us back on our feet until Winston's feeling better and can find another job."

"How much, Catherine?" he asked wearily. He had no intention of granting her request, but he was curious how much she needed *this* time.

"Ten thousand should be enough. Maybe fifteen for good measure."

"Even specialists don't cost ten thousand dollars!"

"No, but we have a house payment due. And our air conditioner has been making a strange noise, and I need to have it checked out. You know how expensive things are these days. Plus, Waylon's car needs new tires. Please, Dad?" she whined. It was unbecoming on a fifty-four-year-old woman. "I know I can always depend on you, and we really do need the help."

"Just like you needed my help to pay for your

house insurance. And your new roof. And Waylon's dental work. And most likely a new pair of *Louboutin* shoes for you."

"Father! How could you say such a thing!" Her huffed reply was indignant.

"You've always been a woman of style, my dear. Just like your late mother."

She wasn't swayed by his endearing tone. "What would Mother say if she knew you were refusing to help me?" she demanded harshly.

Vern didn't answer right away. For once, candor outweighed courtesy. "She would probably ask why it took me so long."

"How could you say such a thing to *me*, your own daughter!" she wailed.

"I'm sorry, Catherine, but I simply cannot help you this time."

"You just don't want to! Admit it. You've never cared for Winston. You want to see him fail. And you think Waylon is lazy. You don't understand that a man with his talent deserves better than some job at a fast-food burger joint! He's looking for an employer who appreciates him and his keen sense of fashion design. He can't settle for a job that's beneath him."

"It's honest work, Catherine. Maybe he and Winston could work the same shift and save on commute expenses."

Catherine's gasp was theatrical. "You did *not* just say that to me!"

"I'm sorry, Catherine. I truly am. But I simply can't help you this time."

"You mean you *won't* help me. You refuse to. Did my brother put you up to this?"

"Unless you went to him first, Lawrence has no idea you're calling."

"Of course I didn't go to him! Not with his holier than thou attitude."

"I wish you and your brother could get along better. You know, one day I won't be here to bridge the gap between the two of you."

"So you always say." Her voice sounded bitter.

Vern drew in a sharp breath. He suddenly knew what he needed to do. There was only one way out of this hole he had dug himself into.

"Very well, Catherine. Have it your way."

"So, you'll lend me the money?"

"I'll have to do some homework first."

"Homework? Aren't you a little old for such?"

"One should never be too old for simple mathematics, my dearest. First, I'll need to add up all the money I've loaned you through the years. Don't worry, I won't charge interest. If the amount I've given you is less than your inheritance, I'll consider giving you a lump sum upfront, and have my will redrawn."

"What?" As her outrage grew, so did the volume of her voice. "What! How-How dare you!"

"It's a simple formula, sweetheart. I don't know why I didn't think of this before."

"You can't do that. That's *my* money!"

Not if I spend it first, he thought to himself. He couldn't bequeath what he didn't have.

Catherine hung up without another word.

"Her mother always coddled her," Vern tsked aloud. He spoke to an empty audience. "And I'm afraid I allowed it to continue. But no more. Even if I had the money to give, I now realize the error of my ways. This ends now."

5

Mama Fowler and her family lived in Muskrat Hollow or, as locals called it, Muskrat Holler. Tucked between the ridges of the Ozark Mountains, the entire holler was inhabited by the family and their extended kinfolk. Unless they had a durn good reason to be there, outsiders weren't welcome.

Willow had explained her intentions of conducting a stakeout. She would record and note everyone who came in and out of the secluded valley. She assured Claudette Fowler that her team would research and confirm every vehicle that entered their domain. If someone was, indeed, stealing from them, they would at least have a suspect pool already in place.

Willow arrived at the homestead at the agreed-upon time and parked under a shade tree.

Homestead was a lofty word for the sad-looking house that stood before her. She decided the old clapboard house was originally painted white. The paint was now faded and peeling, exposing more weathered gray wood than it did color. Add-ons sprouted in every direction to accommodate the ever-expanding family. At one time, the add-on to the add-on must have been scheduled for new paint. Four different colors, all the width of a paint roller, testified to a job unfinished and soon forgotten. Not to mention that someone considered themselves an artist and had painted their rendition of a giant American flag on yet another addition.

Plastic tubs and old tires served as flowerbeds. Weeds tried to choke out the wisteria growing in one tire, but the ivy next to it was determined to thrive. A withering rose bush clung to life inside another tire. Free-range chickens pecked at the unidentified plant sprouting from one of the tubs, and in another, she saw the remains of three tomato stalks. Willow suspected that was marijuana growing in the third and fourth tubs.

She counted at least five dogs in the yard. They looked lazy enough now, but Willow knew the hound dogs would come to life the moment she stepped from her car. She considered them more of a nuisance than a threat, but it was the pit bull that kept her seated in place.

Soon enough, a burly man appeared at her window. She thought his name might be Darrell. Or was it Darnell? He yanked the door open without warning.

"You gonna sit there all day, or you coming with me?"

Claudette insisted that Willow's shiny new car would stick out like a fine stallion among a field of jackasses. If the point of the mission was to go undercover, she had to look the part.

"I—I guess I'm coming with you." The thought

made her uncomfortable, but it came with the job.

He gave a disgruntled look at the satchel she hauled from the car. Inside were her stakeout essentials: notepad, battery bank for her phone, infrared binoculars, bottled water, tissues, snacks. There was a light sweater for cooler temperatures, and a small battery-operated fan for the heat.

He stalked toward a waiting side-by-side. "Get in. I'll take you to the spot."

Willow crawled inside the ATV, wondering where they were going and how she would get back here. Before she could ask, he handed her a two-way radio. "Call when you're ready to come back."

With a lurch, they were off. She could swear he hit every bump and every hole he could find. They kicked up enough dirt to leave a desert naked and her covered in sand. Willow breathed a sigh of relief when Darrell-Darnell stomped on the brake and cut the engine.

"Here we are," he announced.

Willow looked around in confusion. "Where?"

"In your vantage point. Duh."

She didn't appreciate the insinuation she was dumb, but she wisely remained silent.

"No one will suspect you're even here."

"In where?" she asked again. All she saw was a copse of trees and an old pick-up truck. Vines grew around it, and weeds had started to grow in its bed. The rusty red body—rusty was the condition, not the color—was badly dented, with parts falling off. The driver's side door was two-toned green and obviously a replacement. The truck's front tires were rotted or flat. The back ones were missing altogether, with blocks serving as somewhat of a leveling agent. It still listed to one side.

Willow's eyes grew wide. "In *there*?"

"Sure. It's the perfect disguise. No one will even see you, but you can see them."

He pointed to a piece of cardboard as if it were the piece d'resistance. It filled the void where the window glass should have been on the door.

"You seriously expect me to get in *there*?" It was all she could do to keep her voice somewhat civil.

He looked baffled by her question. "Why not?"

"For one thing, I'm sure it's rat infested! Not to mention full of spiders and possibly snakes. Plus, there's cardboard on the window! How am I supposed to see out of that?"

"There's peeky holes in it. See?" He pointed his finger at a half-dozen small holes. Leaning in against the cardboard, he gave her a demonstration. "See? Just scrunch up your eye and look through one of these holes. You can see anything you want."

Her voice was dry. "As long as it's within the line of vision of one of these holes."

Darrell-Darnell took her point into consideration.

"Don't you have anything better than this?" Willow asked.

He contemplated her question for a moment before breaking out in a smile. Snapping his fingers, he said, "I know just the place!"

Willow sighed in relief as she returned to the ATV. She didn't even mind the bumpy ride, not if it saved her from the horrors of the rat mobile.

Soon, her chauffeur lurched to a stop in front of yet another stand of trees.

Her relief was short-lived. "I don't see anything," she protested. A small gasp escaped when she realized the obvious. "Am I sitting on the *ground*? In the dark?" Suddenly, the rat mobile didn't sound quite so horrible.

"No, silly," the man scoffed. "You're sitting up there." When he lifted his arm upward, Willow's eyes followed. His finger pointed toward the sky.

She saw it now. A deer stand perched at least twelve feet in the air, resting on a sturdy limb and further anchored by two long, metal legs. At least it was a box stand, outfitted with a floor and four plywood walls.

The thought of sitting in the decrepit truck or on the ground had been met with something akin to horror. But this time, her voice was more curious than appalled.

"I'm sitting in a deer stand?"

Darrell-Darnell shrugged. In an attempt to be polite, he turned his head away to spit out a stream of tobacco juice. "Why not? You got a bird's eye view of near 'bout the whole holler."

She had to admit that his plan had merit. No one would give a second thought to a deer stand that had obviously been there for several years. Over time, the camo spray paint had faded on the weathering wood. The faint blur of greens and browns looked more natural this way, blending effortlessly into the surrounding foliage.

"How do I get up there?" she asked.

"There's a ladder 'round the backside of the tree."

She followed him around the tree to eye a questionable homemade ladder made of angle iron.

The welded steps were spaced further apart than commercial standards, but they looked sturdy enough. It was the depth of the rungs, the height of the ladder, and the heavy bag on her shoulder that worried her.

Seeing her eye her bag, the big man offered, "Want me to take that up for you?"

His chivalry surprised her. She eagerly accepted, handing him the satchel without hesitation.

The ladder shook with each heavy step he took, but it never bowed. Willow took it as a positive sign.

Darrell-Darnell disappeared inside the box stand, reemerging a minute later. He stomped down the ladder, speaking as he neared the bottom. "Checked it out for you. Sometimes a few critters and insects hunker down in there for the winter but looks like we were the last ones in."

"Oh. That's good," she murmured. Unlike when she saw the rat mobile, the thought never entered her mind. It made sense, though. If it could climb a tree, it could view the stand as a cozy new home. It all depended on how tightly sealed the box was.

The burly man stood there awkwardly as he waited for her to move. His patience wore thin while she visually inspected the stand.

"Are you going up there or not?" he blurted out.

His blunt question spurred her into motion. "I—I'm going." She put her foot on the first wrung. "I was planning to stay until about two. Will that be a problem?"

"No. Just call me on that radio I gave you."

"You won't be asleep?"

"I'm a light sleeper."

She had to take him at his word. She hoisted herself up to the second wrung before asking one last question. "Tell me your name again?"

"Davis."

I was close, she consoled herself. *They all start with a D.*

"Thank you, Davis. I'll radio you when I'm ready to come in."

Willow hesitated at the top of the ladder. She felt intimidated by the boxy deer stand, knowing she would be out here alone and in the dark. The very thought of those 'critters' joining her was almost as frightening as the potential danger of this stakeout. If someone was stealing from Mama Fowler's illegal operation, they wouldn't think twice about eliminating a spy.

As Mama Fowler had explained, it was almost time for shift change. Willow was there, in part, to ensure that everyone who was scheduled to leave at the end of the day actually left the fields. After she had raised the question, there was speculation among the other two dark-haired sons (those two must *surely* be Darrell and Darnell; Joe Ray and Garner were the redheads) that this could be an inside job. Someone on the payroll—the brothers mentioned two new hires in particular—could be hanging around after shift, sneaking back into the fields at dark and helping themselves to the product.

The gate wasn't one of the areas covered by surveillance cameras, but there were guards who monitored it round the clock. There was one other access point into the fields, a narrow trail just wide enough for a vehicle to pass. Willow was stationed up the road from it. If anyone turned off the main road without passing through the gates, she would see them.

As soon as she secured the door behind her, Willow went to work setting up her video equipment. She needed daylight to assemble everything correctly and to find the right angle for recording. A bonus to being so high in the air was that it significantly lessened the chance of a stray headlight reflecting off the camera lens.

For what the camera might miss, she had her pen and notebook handy. She would write brief descriptions of each vehicle and, whenever possible, note the license plate numbers. Once night fell, she had infrared goggles for any unexpected traffic.

The first two hours went by quickly. She didn't have long to wait between setting up and the arrival of the first night-shift workers. They straggled in for almost an hour before the day shift started leaving. A few of those were stragglers, too, followed by the family workers. After that, the road quietened. Darkness moved in, and with it came boredom and, yes, she admitted, a touch of paranoia.

Every noise activated her imagination. A limb would fall, or a tree would creak and groan, but all she heard was a panther climbing stealthily toward her. The wind rustled through tree branches, and she imagined a raccoon coming to join her. The call of night birds were ornery horned owls, ready to swoop in and reclaim their hideout. The sounds of snapping twigs and rustled leaves were someone sneaking up on her. The outcome wouldn't be good.

She was almost grateful when she saw the lights

of a vehicle approaching. It posed a danger of its own—this could very well be the thieves she was there to catch—but it gave her something else to worry about. It was unlikely they would notice her so high up, but there was always a chance their lights caught the lens on her camera.

She slid on her night vision goggles and focused as the vehicle came closer. She couldn't detect the color of the dark vehicle, but she knew it was a pickup truck. Earlier in the day, she had scoured the internet, taking a self-taught crash course on vehicle identification. With mediocre confidence, she decided this one was a Dodge.

Not long afterwards, a delivery van with no signage approached. Its presence didn't surprise her, but she recorded it just the same. She knew the Fowlers had to move their product somehow, and night transport made the most sense.

Only one other vehicle traveled the road that night, a mid-sized SUV in a nondescript, neutral color. She couldn't see the license plate, and there was nothing distinguishable about the vehicle. She saw a hundred just like it on a daily basis.

She watched as all three vehicles eventually left. It was close to one in the morning, and she had another hour of night sounds to endure. Another hour of creeping predators and hidden dangers.

Surveillance in a suburban neighborhood or a store parking lot was one thing; surveillance in a secluded wooded hollow was another.

Claudette Fowler called early the next morning,

before Willow had even crawled out of bed. Everleigh took the call, fending off Claudette's abrasive words.

"We haven't had time to accumulate all the information yet," she assured the older woman. "Once we do, we'll send it to you for confirmation. If there are any vehicles you don't recognize or that weren't authorized to be there, we'll track them down and find out who they are and why they were there."

"Your mama's still sleeping, ain't she?"

Everleigh neither confirmed nor denied her words. "I have the information right here in front of me. I assure you, I'm already working on it."

"See to it that you do. I want that information by noon."

"If possible," Everleigh said in a pleasant tone. She wasn't backing down, no matter how ornery and dangerous the Fowlers reportedly were. "Thank you for calling, Mrs. Fowler. I'll be in touch."

Across the room, her grandmother looked at her over the rim of stylish reading glasses. "Girl, you do know you're dancing with fire."

"I love a good, hot Salsa!" Everleigh grinned, pretending to swish a ruffled Latin skirt.

"I'm serious. The Fowlers are known for bad tempers, bad manners, and bad payback."

"She came to us, not the other way around. She'll get it when she gets it."

"Good thing your mother forwarded it all to you. At least you could say you were working on it."

"I could say it, all right. Doesn't make it true."

"Everleigh!" Ireland chided.

"What?" the redhead asked innocently. "I'm still going through morning emails."

"And social media, no doubt."

"Okay, okay. I'll get to work on it now." She made a show of changing screens and pulling up a new folder. "Does that make you feel better?"

Her grandmother offered a serene smile. "Immensely."

By the time Willow came down, Everleigh had the video edited into a clean copy with sharper details.

"Ah, she lives!"

Willow gave her daughter a bleary-eyed smile. A cup of coffee nestled in her hands. "I forgot how exhausting stakeouts were. It's not just the late hours. It's the boredom and the confinement."

"I can only imagine. I'm sure the silence out there was deafening," Everleigh commiserated.

With an amused smile, Ireland asked, "Have you ever been in the woods at night? I was raised in the woods. Nighttime is when the creatures come out of hiding. It's not as silent as you think. Insects buzzing, night birds calling, wildlife moving, trees creaking. The forest comes alive at night."

"Landee, why are your eyes glowing like that? You look excited by the very thought of it."

"Believe me, child. There's nothing like it! It makes you feel alive."

"Well," Willow said sardonically, "something was alive out there. I could have sworn it was panthers and rabid raccoons and maybe a fire-breathing dragon or two, but I managed to survive."

"From what's on this video, it doesn't look like much happened. Outside your imagination, of course."

"Unless Claudette says otherwise, not much did. I

only saw one questionable vehicle, and it may have been part of their transport team, for all I know."

"What kind was it?"

"An unassuming SUV. It was that last one to arrive, and next-to-last one to leave."

"If I was doing something sneaky like selling raw product for illegal drug use, that's exactly what I'd want," Ireland said. "An unassuming vehicle."

"Even the delivery van was unmarked."

"Which was probably smart," Everleigh said. "Even if it was a dispensary or pharmacy making a legal purchase for medicinal purposes, an unmarked van is less likely to be hijacked."

"That's true. But it still wouldn't be legal," Willow argued. "The Fowlers don't have a grower's permit."

"Which we have to overlook," Ireland reminded them. "Our objective is to find who's stealing their produce."

"Their *illegal* produce," Everleigh couldn't help but point out.

"I'm surprised you didn't flash that in her face when Claudette called this morning."

"She's already called?" Willow groaned as she drained her coffee cup.

Ireland looked somewhat amused. "Crawling in that cup to lick the bottom won't do any good. Here, I'll make you some more," Ireland offered, reaching for the cup. "I'll let your daughter explain her saucy attitude with our client."

"What did you do, Everleigh Renae?"

"Claudette called, barking out orders to have our report to her by noon. I told her she'd get it when she got it." With a shrug, she admitted, "Not in those exact words, but she got the message. I hung up before she could demand anything else."

"We need this case, Everleigh."

"We need respect. She can't just snap her fingers and expect us to dance to her tune. Her family may have to, but not us."

"She *is* our client, you know. We work for her, not the other way around."

"She hired us because of our expertise. She knows we have a reputation for getting results. She has to trust us and give us the time and the space to do our job."

"Convince her, not me."

"We'll do our job the best we can, and she'll just have to accept that. If we miss her noon deadline, so be it."

"But we won't, right?"

Everleigh flashed her megawatt smile. "Nah. I have everything almost done. But just for fun, I may wait until 12:30 or so to send it."

6

Vern scanned the restaurant for his lunch date. He spotted her in the dimly lit corner, already seated at "their table." He hurried over and slipped into the chair across from her.

He flashed his most charming smile. "I hope I didn't keep you waiting too long, my dear."

"No, Vern," Tilly assured him with a smile. "Just long enough to order our usual."'

His smile turned indulgent. "You know me so well, sweetheart. It's no wonder we fit together so nicely." He reached across the table to take her hand. Entwining his fingers with hers, he sounded sincere when he said, "We won't have to keep our relationship secret much longer. I suspect Catherine will pay me a visit soon, and I can tell her the news. I want my children to hear it from me first, before it hits the grapevine. You understand that, don't you, my love?"

"Of course. I know how close she was to her late mother. She may not take the news well."

"Yes, she was very close to Martha, but deep down

I believe my daughter wants to see me happy. And you, Tilly Orbach, make me very happy."

"You always say the most flattering things."

"Flattering, perhaps, but nonetheless true."

Tilly pulled her hand away as the waitress brought their meal.

The doctor took a big bite and pronounced, "The meatloaf is good, but not as good as yours, Tilly."

"You say that every time."

"It's true every time."

Tilly took a sip of her iced tea before timidly returning to their conversation. "I'm anxious to meet Catherine."

"Soon, my dear. Soon," Vern promised. "We have to give her time to adjust to the idea of me with another woman."

"I can understand that, but have you never introduced her to one of your lady friends before?"

"There's never been another friend before," he claimed.

"I find that hard to believe. You're a very... vibrant man, Vern. I'm sure there must have been many before me." Tilly gave him a coy look over the rim of her glasses.

"My Martha was a wonderful woman. It's not been easy finding someone to fill her shoes. But then, I met you."

"You're making me blush."

"Pink is a lovely color on you, my love."

"Eat your meatloaf, Vern, before it gets cold."

They enjoyed the rest of their meal over small talk. Before the waitress returned for their dessert order, Vern consulted his watch.

"My, my. I had no idea it was so late. I lose all track of time while I'm in your delightful company, Tilly!" He sounded almost reproachful. "I'm afraid I'm running late for my afternoon appointments."

"You haven't even had dessert yet!" she protested. She knew how much he loved sweets.

"I'll have to forgo the indulgence today, I'm afraid. Duty calls."

"I could bring a pie over this evening, if you'd like," Tilly offered.

"No, no. That won't be necessary!" Realizing how sharp his voice came out, he quickly offered a reasonable excuse. "Thank you, but I have this honey cake you made for me. I'll limit myself to just one slice on the way back to the office, so that I can have the rest this evening."

"You probably shouldn't eat it all in one evening," Tilly cautioned. "It's sweet, you know."

"The sweeter, the better. Just like you." He motioned for the waitress to bring their check. He paid the bill and escorted Tilly to her car. It, too, was parked at the rear of the lot, secluded from open view.

"Until next time, my love." He made the promise as he pulled her into a long embrace. "Soon, we won't have to meet like this. We can eat right there in Lime Creek for all to see. I just need to speak to Catherine first and make certain I have her blessing before I make our relationship public. You do understand, don't you, Tilly?" He tilted her chin upward so he could gaze into her eyes.

"I understand completely, Vern," she assured him.

He chuckled and brazenly patted her backside.

"That's my girl."

Another whispered endearment in her ear, then he was gone. Tilly watched as he drove away.

She definitely had a secret. A delightfully daring secret.

Secret or not, Tilly pulled out her phone and sent a text.

Claudette called again that afternoon. Everleigh decided to play nice, given that the impatient woman had waited several hours before demanding answers.

"Mrs. Fowler, I'm so glad you called. I just finished compiling the information. If you give your email address, I'll send you the file."

"That's not good enough. Bring it to me," the older woman snapped.

Everleigh rolled her eyes but remained calm. "Would tomorrow morning work for you?"

"In an hour would work for me! Look, Missy, I waited all day like you asked. I ain't bothered you, now have I? Now it's your turn to do what I ask."

"I can't be there in an hour, Mrs. Fowler. It takes that long just to drive there."

"Fine. I'll see you in two hours." She hung up before Everleigh could protest.

Slamming down the phone, she fumed, "The nerve of that woman!"

"What's wrong?" Willow asked.

"She demanded I bring her the information this afternoon. In two hours! Then she hung up before I could say anything!"

"Looks like you're going to Muskrat Holler," her

mother teased.

"I refuse to be at that woman's beck and call."

"She's our client. That's our job."

"Our job is to get results, not be her puppet."

Willow reached for her purse. "Come on, puppet. I'll go with you if that makes you feel any better."

"What about Laura Beth? I can't just leave her at school all evening."

"She's already planning to go with Landee today, remember? They're going to bake cookies."

Everleigh grumbled, "Whose side are you on, anyway?"

"In this instance, the client's, I'm afraid. Besides, look at it this way. The sooner we solve this case, the sooner we're done with it. And with the Fowlers."

Everleigh still wasn't happy about it. "Fine," she sniffed. "But you're driving."

Her reaction to seeing the Fowler house was the same as her mother's had been. With a mixture of trepidation, skepticism, and a touch of awe that such a monstrosity existed, Everleigh could only stare.

"They have dogs," Willow warned.

"Will they bite?"

"No clue. Dar—uhm, Davis," she corrected herself, "came out and met me."

Everleigh peered toward the door. "Look. There's someone now."

"That's one of the daughters-in-law."

"Does *she* bite? She doesn't look too friendly."

"Get used to it."

Everleigh reluctantly opened her door. It seemed to act as a silent alarm to activate the many dogs.

"Dogs! Sit!" the woman ordered. With that, she

turned to go back into the house. Her gracious invitation for them to follow was a simple hitch of her thumb.

They followed behind, entering a messy living room where two teenagers barely paused in their make-out session to acknowledge their presence. A younger tween sat in front of the television, randomly flipping through channels. He stopped on a bra commercial featuring two buxom women.

There were two tables stuffed into the dining room, making the room feel cramped. Willow supposed it took every seat and more to accommodate the whole family. They skirted around the tables to enter the kitchen.

Claudette Fowler reigned at the head of the kitchen table, with three of her sons already seated. To her right, an empty seat had been reserved for Willow. Seeing that she hadn't come alone, the son on the left vacated his chair. In a show of hierarchy, he unceremoniously dumped his brother from the next chair, bumping him further down the line.

The proper protocol extended only to familial power. None of the men were chivalrous enough to stand as their guests took their seats. Nor did anyone bother with a greeting.

Claudette cut to the chase. "Let's see it." She held out her hand for the file. "Georgia, bring us all some coffee." She didn't ask if anyone other than herself wanted any. Coffee it was.

Everleigh gave her the manila envelope. "I'm Everleigh, one of the partners with *Intuitive Investigations.*" She addressed the other woman with a steady gaze, miffed for not being acknowledged.

Claudette returned the gaze. There was a slight challenge in her eyes. "I know who you are. I never go into a deal without studying my opponent."

"We're not your opponent. You hired us for our expertise, which is exactly what you'll get." She nodded to the envelope in Claudette's hands. "I think you'll find everything you asked for. You'll see shift change is first. We noted the arrival and departure of each vehicle. We're making the assumption that your guards recognized and approved each one as it passed."

"You sure speak fancy, don't you?" The red-haired man grinned. "You may have to dumb it down for my brothers."

"Hey! I resent that." A dark-haired brother slapped him upside the head.

"We're guessing your guards okayed them," Everleigh rephrased. She flipped her laptop open and pulled up a digital file.

"These are pictures of the three vehicles that came through after hours. Do you recognize them?"

Claudette examined them without comment. She gestured for Everleigh to turn the screen toward her sons.

When all three men followed their mother's lead of no comment, Willow stared at them incredulously. "Seriously? None of you have any comments?"

As always, Claudette spoke for her family. "We know 'em. They have reason to be there."

"So, they're customers?" Everleigh asked. "Is the van part of your distribution team?"

"All you need to know is that they have reason to be there."

Everleigh's patience had grown thin. "Look, Mrs. Fowler. You hired us to find your thief. We have to know who's who. If someone is a customer, they are either a) helping themselves to the product, or b) paying with bad money. You haven't mentioned counterfeit bills, so I'm assuming that's not the case. If they're part of your distribution team, they are either a) skimming off the top, or b) making partial deliveries and keeping the rest for themselves."

"If you want us to help you, you have to help us," Willow urged.

"All you need to know is that we recognize these vehicles," Mama Fowler said stubbornly. "They had reason to be there, and they checked in at the guard shack."

"Listen." Everleigh tried again, her voice firmer this time. "It's no secret that your family grows weed. I know it. You know it. My twelve-year-old daughter even knows it! My guess is that the local law enforcement knows it, too, but they let it slide for reasons unimportant for now. The point is, there's no reason for you to try to hide your operation from us. We knew the crop you were talking about, and we took the case anyway. So, make all our lives easier and just cut out the pretense. If these were your delivery drivers, just say so. We'll check them out and potentially save you from losing even more money."

Mama Fowler didn't bother consulting her sons. They all knew she called the shots.

"Those three vehicles had every right to be there because, yes, they were picking up deliveries. Are you satisfied?" She glared at the younger woman.

"It's a start."

"You're a sassy one, ain't ya?" There was a hint of begrudging respect in her voice.

Everleigh tossed her red curls. "I got it from my mother, who got it from her mother."

"How is Irie, anyway?" The older woman knew Ireland by her 'mountain' name. Growing up in Dalton Holler, everyone had called her by the adaptation.

"As feisty and opinionated as ever," Willow assured her. "Next time, we'll make sure to bring her with us."

"She might not want to come slumming with you, you know. It might mess with her fancy new lifestyle."

"Obviously, you don't know my grandmother." Everleigh sniffed.

"How could I? She don't even visit her kinfolk."

"We didn't come here to discuss my grandmother. We came to discuss your case. We'll need the name of these and all your distributors."

When Claudette would have protested, Willow reiterated, "Mrs. Fowler, we can't do our job without those names."

Georgia returned with the coffee. As she served it, her mother-in-law instructed, "Georgia, get these ladies the file on our distribution team."

"All of them, Mama?" There was a flicker of concern in her eyes.

"That's right. All of our scheduled distribution sources." A solemn look passed between the two women.

Willow would have asked about it, but the third brother interrupted. "Are you sure about this,

Mama?"

"We hired them to help, Darnell. We gotta let them help."

A few minutes later, Georgia returned with the requested file. "Here's a list of our distributors."

"And the vehicles they drive?" Willow asked.

"Included." She looked none too happy about it.

"You'll need to verify the list we gave you. Pay special attention to whether or not they cleared your checkpoints. No one turned off the main road, but I couldn't see the gate from where I sat."

Darnell took offense. "You tellin 'us how to do our jobs?"

"No. I'm asking you to help us do ours."

"Then what are we paying *you* for?" Darrell, the other dark-haired man, demanded.

Everleigh lifted her chin and answered, "We'll work the client and delivery angle, you work the employee angle. Ruling these out will be easier than ruling out other possibilities."

"And that's what?" Georgia asked.

"An outside threat. That option leaves literally thousands of possibilities. So, let's start with our known potential suspects and work from there."

Mama Fowler stood, signaling their meeting was over. She didn't bother with a goodbye, nor a thank you. All she said was, "Georgia, make sure the dogs behave."

Everleigh wondered what Georgia's surly expression was about as she walked them to the door. Calling it such was a stretch. She went well ahead and waited for them to catch up, but at least she held the door open for them.

She refused, however, to step out of the way for Everleigh to pass. Their shoulders couldn't help but touch, and in that instant, Everleigh knew what the problem was. Georgia Fowler was jealous. She didn't like the way her husband had looked at her. She suspected it might be a thing with gingers. Maybe they were attracted to their own. Joe Ray wasn't the smartest man on the planet, but he was her man. Georgia wasn't about to lose him to some woman who wore expensive shoes and used big, fancy words.

Everleigh felt the sentiment as surely as if the other woman said it aloud.

This city girl better watch her back, or I will gladly take her down.

Once in the car, Everleigh watched as the house appeared smaller and smaller in the rearview mirror. Sarcasm lay heavy in her voice. "That was fun."

"I'm glad you're so easily entertained. Next time, I'll send you in alone."

"Georgia might devour me whole."

"Her hostility was directed at you, but I felt the steam from where I sat. She thinks you're after her man."

Everleigh snorted. "If I ever get mixed up with that bunch, shoot me on the spot."

The words had hardly left her lips. An actual gun shot rang out, and both women jumped.

Everleigh's unruly curls grazed the roof when she jerked upright. "What was that?"

Willow's voice was shaky. "Exactly what you think! Someone just shot at us."

"Where did it come from?" Everleigh's head pivoted back and forth as she searched their surroundings.

"I don't know, but it hit the dirt in front of us. It was a warning shot."

"Of what?" her daughter cried.

"Not to ask so many questions? Not to get too close? Not to double-cross them?" Willow guessed. "I have no clue, but they made one thing clear. Tread lightly."

"Tread lightly, don't ask questions, use only the information they parcel out in small batches, resist the overwhelming charm of their menfolk, ignore their illegal activities, keep our heads low, but find the dirty snake who dares to steal from them." Everleigh counted their duties on her fingers with exaggerated movement. "Does that cover it?"

"Just about."

"What do they think we are? Magicians?"

"No, but they may mistake us for seers. Many people don't understand that there are vast differences in our gifts."

Some people called their innate ability witchcraft. Some called it magic. Others called it foolishness, simply the power of suggestion. Still others, particularly here in the mountains, saw it as the gift that it was.

'The touch' wasn't just for healing. For Ireland, the gift of persuasion by touch came with heavy responsibility. It couldn't be used for evil or personal gain. If her intentions were pure, she could persuade people to see things in a different light. As an empath, Everleigh used her version of the touch to feel what others felt. She didn't just understand their motivations and personal convictions. She *felt* them.

Willow's talent didn't involve 'the touch.' She wasn't a seer. She couldn't predict the future. But she 'had the knowing' as old-timers called it. She could sense what was, and what was yet to come.

Their unique talents were part of a strange phenomenon among Ireland's maternal people. For generations, during her twentieth year, a daughter who possessed 'the gift' gave birth to a girl child of her own. That child would also possess a unique gift. And when the daughter turned twenty, she, too, would give birth to a gifted girl child.

"Mama Fowler knew Landee from way back when. She knows about our family. She may think I'm a seer and can lead her directly to their thief, but it doesn't work that way," Willow said. "I feel negative and positive energy, so I know something is about to happen, but I don't know what. Just because I sense danger, I don't always know where it's coming from."

"I don't have your particular gift, but even I know where this latest danger comes from. Bullets!"

Willow wasn't convinced. "Actually," she said, "I don't think so. The Fowlers are hunters. They know how to shoot. If they had wanted to hit us, I have no doubt they would have. I think this was nothing more than a reminder of who we're working with, and what they're capable of."

"Okay, so that's where the danger is coming from! Our newest clients."

Her mother frowned. "On that, I do agree."

7

"Ah, Erma, you do know the way to a man's heart." The good doctor pushed his empty plate away and stretched back in his chair. "That, my dear, was absolutely delectable! One of your best recipes yet."

"You're always so good to me, Vern, allowing me to try new recipes out on you before they go on the menu."

"The pleasure is mine, I can assure you."

"The trouble is you never give anything other than glowing praise." Oddly enough, the cook from *The Goose and Gander Diner* frowned.

His belly shook as he chuckled. "And that's a bad thing?"

"It's not that I don't like the compliments. It's just that sometimes, I need constructive criticism."

"Even when there's nothing to criticize?"

"What about the roasted potato medley?" She motioned to the dish in question.

"I admit, I'm not accustomed to what you called purple potatoes. The color of the flesh was surprising, but they have a distinct flavor, don't they? Earthy.

Together with the petite red skins and Yukon golds, I thought it was delightful."

"And the seasoning? You didn't find it too overpowering?" She watched his face closely for his reaction.

"My first thought was that it was slightly bitter," he admitted, "but once I bit into the potatoes, it blended quite nicely."

"You're sure?"

"Would you like for me to have a third helping, just to prove I'm being sincere?"

"I suppose two helpings is testimony enough," she decided. A pleased smile lifted the corners of her severe mouth.

"I'm sorry, my sweets, but I have nothing negative to say about the meal." He lifted upturned palms and offered her a helpless smile. "You are an excellent cook. You've never fed me a meal that wasn't delicious."

He caught one of her hands and pulled her into his lap. "What I'd like to know is what you're serving for dessert."

"Vern!" She playfully swatted his hands. "The things you say!"

"The things I do," he countered, nuzzling her neck. "Or shall I say, the things I'd like to do."

"I'm a lady, Vernon Dudley, and don't you forget it!" She sounded so much sterner than her eyes suggested.

"You, my dearest, are a woman."

The kitchen door rattled as someone attempted to open it. Vern practically dumped Erma onto the floor as he jumped hastily to his feet.

"Vern!" she protested. "What on earth!"

"I-I'm sorry. I was just so startled. I'm not expecting company this evening." He darted his eyes toward the door nervously. What night was it? Had he gotten his dates mixed up? He was entertaining Erma tonight and would make an 'urgent house call' to Sally's tomorrow night. He made it a rule to never dally with a woman on the Lord's Day. Besides, he needed two nights to recuperate before seeing Emmaline on Monday. Especially with all the work he had to do.

The door rattled again, more forcefully this time. Vern straightened his shirt and ran a hand over his hair. He couldn't have any wayward locks giving away his recent overtures.

"Father, are you in there?"

"It's my daughter!" he hissed. "Please, don't say a word. She-She doesn't know about us. She's overly protective and may not take this well."

Erma pressed her lips together in a stern line, but she nodded. With jerky movements, she began clearing the table.

"Coming, dear!" Vern called as he hurried to the door. He opened it, greeting his daughter with what sounded like delight. "To what do I owe this pleasure? I wasn't expecting you."

What he meant was he hadn't expected her so soon. He knew she would come. When whining over the phone didn't work, she always came to plead her case in person.

"Why was the deadlock bolted?" Catherine demanded. "Trying to keep your only daughter out?"

"Of course not, sweetheart. I must have locked it

out of habit."

"Why? Nothing ever happens in this dead horse town!" she complained.

She came up short when she saw a strange woman standing in her father's kitchen. "Who are you?" she demanded.

"I'm Erma." She shot a worried look toward the doctor.

"Erma is the cook I was telling you about," Vern said smoothly. "She comes a few times a month and cooks for me. You know how I am. I get so involved in my work, I sometimes forget to eat."

Catherine eyed his expanding waistline. "I've never known you to miss a meal, and I'm certain you never mentioned hiring a cook."

"I didn't?" He feigned surprise. "I guess that was your brother I told. At any rate, Erma has been a Godsend to this forgetful old man."

"You have the memory of an elephant," Catherine retorted. He knew what she referred to when she added, "Especially when it comes to counting past transgressions."

Erma nervously wiped her hands on a dishtowel. "Why don't you two visit in the living room while I clean up this mess? I'll let myself out when I'm done."

"That's not necessary," Vern protested.

Catherine thought otherwise. "Of course it is. That's what you pay her for, isn't it? What's the point in having a cook, if you have to clean up after her?"

With a helpless look over his shoulder, Vern followed his daughter from the room. Erma glared at his retreating form but said nothing.

The moment they stepped into the other room,

Catherine demanded, "Who is that woman?"

"I told you. She's my part-time cook. She works at *The Goose & Gander Diner* just across the state line, but her talents far exceed a run-of-the-mill diner. Erma could easily be the chef in her own restaurant. I consider myself incredibly fortunate to have her prepare meals for me. Would you care to try some of her dishes? I normally freeze what's left, but I'll happily share."

"Don't pretend she's merely your cook! I saw the look that passed between you. and I see that smear of lipstick—" She reached out to swipe it off her father's cheek, "—right. There."

"I'm planning a dinner for some of my colleagues," he lied smoothly, "and I asked her to cater it. She was thanking me for the opportunity."

Catherine's eyebrows raised in skepticism "What about the woman I saw you with in Branson?"

"I told you. She worked at the clinic a few years ago, and we still keep in touch from time to time. Please, dear, have a seat."

She made no comment. It was obvious she didn't believe him.

As her father seated himself in a comfortable arm chair, Catherine paced the room. She whirled around suddenly and glared at him.

"You have money to wine and dine women, and to have them cook for you. Yet you won't loan money to your only daughter?"

"Are you suggesting I go hungry, so that I can loan you yet more money?"

"That's unfair to say, and you know it! I'm hardly suggesting that you go hungry. I'm simply asking for a loan until Winston can find a proper job."

"There are jobs out there, Catherine, even if he thinks they are beneath him. Sometimes, a man has to do what a man has to do." Vern stared off in space, his thoughts on the debt he still had to pay. Dipping into the trust fund was the only way. He was still the owner, and, as such, had full access to the account. An extra delivery or two, and he should have more than enough.

While his daughter ranted about the unfairness of it all, he mentally calculated how much product he had in stock. He normally sold it processed and ready for consumption, but perhaps he should consider selling off some of his raw product.

"Are you even listening to me?" Catherine demanded.

"Oh, yes, yes. Certainly. Waylon needs braces. But isn't he a bit old for that? Corrective measures are normally taken in one's youth."

Catherine's sigh was audible. "He has his father's mouth. The Jensons are known for their mouths being too crowded for their teeth." The distraction worked. Catherine spent the next several minutes railing against the inferior traits passed down from her husband's family.

It gave Vern time to project the financial benefits of squeezing in another delivery before Wednesday. It would be tricky, but he thought he could manage.

Eventually, Catherine circled back to the reason for her visit.

She planted her hands on her hips and stared him down. "Are you going to give me the money, or not?"

"My lawyer is currently out of town. I can't have

him restructure my will until he returns."

"You're seriously going through with this?" Her look was incredulous. He had never denied her before. Her father always catered to her tears. "You'd actually take my inheritance from me? The money my mother intended for me to have?"

"I'm not taking it from you, Catherine. I'm merely giving it to you early."

"I can't believe you're being so unreasonable! So cruel."

"I'm sorry, Catherine, but it's the only fair thing to do. You've taken your inheritance in installments. Lawrence will get his in a lump sum upon my death."

"He's always been your favorite!" she accused bitterly.

"That is not true. I'm simply trying to be fair to both of you."

Catherine glared at her father; her eyes were full of fire and her voice full of venom.

"I hate you," she proclaimed.

"I'm sorry to hear that, Catherine." His voice remained steady. The doctor was accustomed to her temper tantrums.

"You'll be sorry, Father. I swear, I'll never speak to you again!"

"Catherine, dear, you're being unreasonable."

"You'll never see your grandchildren again, either. I'll see to it that you don't!"

"Your continued threats won't work, Catherine. I've made up my mind, and that's that."

She stared at him again, her expression one of utter disbelief. He was serious. He was refusing to help her, and for once, she couldn't change his mind.

Catherine spat out a final declaration. "You are dead to me. Do you hear me? You. Are. Dead. To me."

"I'm sorry you feel that way. Sadly, I can't buy your love, and I'm through trying."

Catherine grabbed her purse from where she had thrown it. Her hopes for swaying his opinion were dead.

If only he were! she thought bitterly. He hadn't changed his will yet. She would still get her full inheritance if he were to die now.

"I hope you die," she lashed out. "I hope you get hit by a truck. Shot by a jealous husband. Have a heart attack from all the sweets your lady friends bring you."

Seeing the surprise on his face, she smirked. "That's right. I know all about your illicit affairs, Father. I know you're a philanderer and that you use women for your own pleasure. You are despicable, and you deserve whatever fate you're dealt."

She turned back one last time before she stormed from the room.

"Goodbye, Father."

Those were the last words she ever said to him.

With his daughter gone—most likely for good, or at least until she needed another favor—Vern returned to the kitchen. He hadn't had dessert yet, leaving his craving for sweets unquenched. He opened the refrigerator and surveyed his choices. There was the rhubarb pie Erma had put away untouched, thanks to Catherine's interruption. The berry pie from Lucille, minus two slices. There were canapes from Midge, some fancy creation with edible flowers used for decoration and stirred into the frosting. Her daughter was in culinary school, and Vern was always more than happy to give her an amateur but well-cultivated critique.

The doctor couldn't decide between them all, so the logical choice was to make himself a sampler plate. With a half piece of each pie and two canapes, he could enjoy them all.

He had the desserts with a glass of cold milk. As he cleaned up after himself, he realized all that sugar had his heart rattling in his chest. He felt jumpy. Perhaps he should take a nice, long bath. The warm water should calm him down.

He could watch television after that or read. Either one was apt to make him sleepy after a warm bath.

Yet, he wasn't ready to go to bed. He felt oddly energetic. What better time to work down in his basement? He sorely needed to, if he planned to make extra deliveries this week.

Vern whistled a tune as he worked. He would call his financial planner first thing in the morning. If he could free up some funds from the trust, plus drop off a few more shipments, he should have enough to meet Boss' demands.

If there was one thing he knew, it was that Boss didn't like being ignored. He was the sort of man who said 'frog', and the world around him jumped. The loan shark was legendary for his harsh treatment of those who dared to defy him. Few lived to tell about it, but if they did, their disfigurements served as a vivid reminder to others who might be so foolish.

He was quite proud of himself as he finished a

batch of ointments and neatly packed them into a box. Still feeling jittery, however, Vern was trying to decide between calling it a night and preparing one more batch for delivery when his telephone rang. It seemed like a sign, so he pulled off his gloves and answered.

"Dr. Dudley?" The familiar voice sounded timid on the other end of the line.

"Hilda, is that you, my dear?"

"Yes. Yes, it is." She also sounded nervous.

"Well, now, this is a pleasant surprise. How are you doing, sweet Hilda?"

"Well, that's the thing." He could practically hear the way she twisted the phone cord around her finger. She still used a land line for service. He imagined she sat in her leather wingback chair, calling him from the phone between it and her late husband's matching recliner. Burton Dunway had passed away just last year, leaving behind a wife twenty years his junior. During the day, managing their thriving trucking empire kept her busy, but Vern knew she grew lonely in the evenings. "My sciatica is bothering me something awful, Doc. I was wondering…"

"You've already used the balm I gave you?" At fifty-four dollars a jar, *gave* wasn't the right word.

"I'm afraid so. I've been in such pain," she explained. "I know you only make it in small batches, but I'd like to double my order if I can."

"As a matter of fact, I just finished a batch this evening."

"Really?" Her voice brightened at the news.

"Yes. In fact, I planned to call you next week and

ask if I should reserve a jar for you."

Eagerness, perhaps greediness, moved into her words. "How much did you make?"

"It produced eighteen jars. I'm not sure when I'll be able to make more, which is why—"

"I'll take them all!" Hilda interrupted.

Taken by surprise, Vern ran his hand over his beard as he quickly calculated in his head. Eighteen jars at fifty-four dollars apiece...

"I'll pay you a thousand dollars!" She, too, had done the math and knew he would come out ahead.

"Hilda, dear, are you sure?" He tried not to sound too eager. He had enough product to make twice that, but she needn't know that. Every thousand would help.

"Yes, yes. I—I know it's asking a lot, Vern, but I was hoping... That is, with my back hurting this way, I'm not sure I can drive. Is there—Is there any way you could bring it to me? I know it's late, and it's quite an inconvenience, but I'll pay you for your time, of course."

Hilda lived over the state line in Arkansas, where cannabis was restricted to medical use only. While chronic sciatica was a recognized medical condition, strict limits remained on allocations, both per person and per product specifications.

For Hilda, neither limit was sufficient.

Vern's products were known for their generous, not-so-legal amounts of marijuana. He sold it to patients in the form of oils and salves and labeled it as all-natural ingredients. That much was true. It was the high level of concentration that made it illegal. That was why he offered it to only select patients, why he kept it under strict lock and key in his office, and why he produced it himself in his basement laboratory.

And why, at almost eleven o'clock at night, one of his patients begged for home delivery.

His reply wasn't immediate, prompting her to blurt out a new offer. "I'll pay you fifteen hundred dollars," she said, "plus another two hundred for delivery. That's seventeen hundred dollars. In cash."

"I can hear the pain in your voice, dear Hilda." His voice was gentle and full of compassion. "I'll leave within the half hour."

"Thank you, Vern. Thank you. I'll be ever so grateful."

"Anything for you, my dear. I know how you suffer."

Vern closed down his equipment, tidied up, swept the floor, and turned off the lights. With the room once again spotless, he carried the boxed jars with him as he climbed the stairs. He left the house soon after that, eager to collect the payout.

He congratulated himself as he drove into Arkansas.

Not bad for an evening's work, my man.

Hilda Dunway lived in one of Harison's upscale neighborhoods. It was late by the time he arrived, but she met him with renewed energy. He suspected she had nibbled on her edibles before he arrived.

"I can't thank you enough for making this special house call," she told him as she led the way into the living room. "I hated to ask, but I was in such excruciating pain!"

"You seem to be feeling better than earlier. That's

comforting to hear." He placed the box of salves on the coffee table.

"I took something to help with the pain, but it *will* come back." She spoke with confidence.

"I wish there was more I could do. Unfortunately, sciatica is a chronic condition with little recourse."

"At least the salve helps. I'm so glad I discovered it. I just wish it was easily obtainable here in Arkansas."

"It's my own formula," he reminded her. "I make it in my private lab to assure product control and quality."

Hilda lifted her wine glass to her lips. He suspected the wine may have contributed to her good mood, as well. Swirling the liquid with a casual twist of her wrist, there was nothing casual about the way she studied him. Making himself at home, the doctor had taken a seat on the other end of the sofa. "Tell me, Vern," she said. "Have you considered expanding your distribution? I think you have a goldmine on your hands, but you aren't taking advantage of its full potential."

"That's an intriguing thought, Hilda, but I'm afraid I don't have the resources, nor the personnel, to expand at this time."

She suddenly realized she was drinking alone. "Oh, Heavens! Where are my manners! Would you care for some wine? Something stronger?"

"Wine would be delightful, but only a little. I'm driving."

"Let me get you a glass."

"No, no. You stay where you are and get comfortable. I know where the glasses are."

There was a small but well-stocked bar in one corner of the room. He brought back a long-stemmed glass and another pre-chilled bottle of wine from the cooler.

"Please, polish off the bottle," Hilda encouraged. "I have something I'd like to discuss with you."

"Very well." He did as she suggested before settling into the cushions. "I'm listening."

"My Burton was a brilliant businessman, and he left me with a more than generous bank account. I'm always looking for a good investment opportunity, and I believe you have the products I could back. What I'm proposing, Vern, is a business deal between us."

Vern held up a staying hand. "Having your full confidence is a true honor, dear Hilda. But please understand. While I conform to strict standards, my products are not FDA approved."

"I'm aware of that. Many lotions, vitamins, and natural remedies aren't. I dare say that most, in fact, aren't. That doesn't concern me in the least."

"When I first suggested you try *Live Again* lotion, I explained that one of the reasons it works so well is that it's professional grade. Normally, you would need a prescription to get something of this quality and strength."

They both knew that even then it exceeded the legal limits.

They both ignored the truth.

"I'm well aware of that. But I have... connections..." she chose her words with care, "who would be happy to share your products with others. And better yet, I have the logistic resources to transport and deliver the products anywhere we'd like."

His heart leaped at the opportunity, but reality weighed heavy in his stomach.

"While the thought is most exhilarating, I'm afraid I don't have a facility capable of producing the volume we're talking about."

"What if you built a new one?"

"Sadly, that's not financially possible."

"What if it were?"

"In that case, I would consider it. However, it simply is beyond my reach at this time."

"I'm willing to put it within your reach." Her eyes were bright with intent. Her voice was purposeful. Hilda leaned forward, all traces of intoxication gone. "I want to invest in your products, Vern. I will build you whatever facility you need."

"I—I..." He was at a loss for words. "I have no employees," he blurted out. "And I couldn't possibly manage it on my own."

"We'll hire however many employees you need. We can build the laboratory to your exact specifications. Hire the workers you need. Adhere to your standards and your formulations. You'll be in charge of everything, Vern. Everything but the bankroll. That, Vern, will be my contribution to the partnership."

The doctor's mind was spinning. Before he could even consider such a grand production, he would need more suppliers. He bought the raw product directly from two growers, but it wouldn't be enough.

And where would this facility be? Missouri would be the most logical choice. Their drug laws weren't as strict as Arkansas', and it would be closer for him. But again, *where*? There would be paperwork. Red tape. Government standards. Approval from the state. The formula he used would still be illegal.

"We must be reasonable. In order to conform to government requirements, we would have to change the formula," he pointed out.

Hilda raised her eyebrows, a faint smirk on her lips. When the beautiful young woman married the homely, much older Burton Dunway, everyone assumed she was looking for a father figure. But Vern knew she was more than her lush figure and charming smile suggested. Hilda was a cunning businesswoman, and she was instrumental in building the Dunway empire. She also knew how to close deals.

She leaned forward now, exposing a generous view of her impressive cleavage. "Who said anything about government requirements?" she purred.

"You do realize what you're proposing." It wasn't exactly a question. "Let's be frank. The formula I use is beyond legal limits. Unless we lower the ingredients, the product itself will be illegal."

She maintained eye contact with the doctor, her eyes deceptively innocent. "And your point?"

A slow smile spread across both their faces. For the first time since Wednesday, Vern felt more than simply hopeful. He felt confident.

"I'll need to secure another supplier, perhaps two. Sometimes negotiating a deal can be time consuming. And expensive."

"I think I might be able to speed things up."

Hilda stood, a slight wince on her face. She truly

did suffer from sciatica. Her legs were slightly wobbly as she made her way toward the bar. Given the unopened bottle on the table, Vern wondered why she stepped behind it, until she turned halfway back and smiled coyly. She reached for the edge of an ornate frame housing a vineyard-themed painting and tugged. It swung forward to reveal a home safe.

When she returned to the sofa, she carried a thick stack of one-hundred-dollar bills. She fanned the end with her thumb, emphasizing just how thick it was. "I'm confident you can broker a deal in no time at all."

Mesmerized with the flutter of all those magnificent bills, he distractedly murmured, "I feel confident that I can."

"Shall we drink to our new partnership?" She nodded to the other bottle of wine.

"Regretfully, I'm driving," he reminded her.

"It's already late. You're welcome to stay."

Vern was tempted, but he had to say no.

"I have to be at the clinic early in the morning. I'm afraid I really must go."

"I do understand. I, too, have to be at the office." When she stood, she once again grimaced.

"Don't see me out. I suggest a warm shower, a generous slathering of salve, and a good night's sleep."

"Thank you again for coming so late, Vern. I really did need the salve."

"Absolutely."

"I'd like to hand samples out to potential clients, to get them as enthused as I am about this project."

"That's a splendid idea. I'll order small jars and vials to give away."

"Perfect! I'm so excited about our new business venture!"

When she threw her arms around him in a hug, Vern almost changed his mind about staying. He and Hilda had always maintained a doctor/patient relationship, but tonight held promise of something more. Not just a business alliance, but perhaps a personal one, as well.

There was no doubt Hilda was a beautiful and vibrant woman, but Vern knew his limitations. It wasn't just the physical aspect; he was eighty-three years old, after all. But it went deeper than that. Yes, he was a man who loved the company of a woman. He craved the gentle nature they embodied. He loved how they moved, how they smelled, how their skin felt when he touched them. He enjoyed their kisses and warm embraces, but that was all. In his heart, he was still married to his beloved Martha. Even a womanizer such as him couldn't betray his late wife's memory in such a way.

As tempted as he was to stay, he knew he would leave. Aside from his loyalty to Martha, there was something more tempting than a night in Hilda's arms. He could hardly wait to reach his car and count the money.

With Wednesday looming large, his life could depend on it.

8

The Community Clinic and Urgent Care Center was Lime Creek's best alternative for medical care. The other choices were at least a half hour's drive to a hospital, or an hour or more to a decent trauma center. Most people reserved those options for specialists and hospitals.

Dr. Vern Dudley was one of three general practitioners at the clinic, and by far the busiest. He had a robust clientèle that ranged from babies to Old Mel Helberger.

The doctor ushered his current patient from the examining room, walking her to the front desk. This sort of extra attention was just one of the many things that endeared him to his patients. Not only did he listen to them, but he took a genuine interest. True, he was most interested in his feminine clients, but he afforded men and women alike the same courtesy of seeing them out.

"It was good to see you again, Justine. You take care of that toe, and you let me know if it gives you any more trouble." He winked playfully as he jested,

"Especially if it keeps you from baking another one of your mouth-watering pies."

Justine Paul giggled as her cheeks turned a darker shade of orange-red. She was given to a ruddy complexion as it was, but when she blushed, her cheeks took on an orange glow that clashed with her hair. Once-fiery red, gray had now taken hold, fading it to a muddy, murky orange.

"Thank you, Dr. Dudley. And I won't hesitate to call if it comes to that."

"Good, good." He handed her file to the young woman behind the desk. "Raley, will you take care of our lovely lady, here?"

"Certainly, Doctor." Raley Bumgartner kept the smirk from showing on her face. Inwardly, she kept a silent count. That was the fifth time he had used the words 'our lovely lady' today, and the afternoon had just begun. Not to mention the fact that only one of the women even came remotely close to fitting the description.

Nonetheless, Raley ignored her observations and forced the sound of respect into her voice. "Your next patient is waiting for you in Room 5, sir."

"Thank you, Raley." Dr. Dudley retraced his steps, stopping in front of the furthest examining room. He skimmed the patient's folder as he walked through the door.

"Well, now. This is a surprise," he told the man seated inside. "We did your three-month checkup just a few weeks ago. Are you not feeling well today, Mel?"

Mel was the oldest citizen in the county, clocking in at a robust ninety-nine years young. Most impressive was the fact that he still lived at home and was still driving. His 1948 Ford F-1 pickup truck didn't go over forty miles an hour, which suited Mel—and the local police—just fine. Given that the ancient machine overheated after thirty miles, his driving exploits were confined to Lime Creek, another thing that suited Mel. Since all of his friends and most of his family had gone on before him, he didn't have much use for the outside world these days. He was happy puttering around in his garden, tending to his farm animals, and working crossword puzzles.

"I don't know why you insist I come so dad-burn often," the old man grumbled. "You sure you ain't runnin' some kind of insurance scam, Doc?" He was only half teasing.

"No scam, Mel," the doctor assured him with a chuckle. "Like I always tell you, I like keeping tabs on my best advertisement. Having a healthy patient all these years looks good on my resume." He winked in good nature; he, too, was only half teasing.

"No thanks to that no-taste diet you tried shovin' down my throat. I been eatin' my eggs fried in bacon grease for as long as I can remember. Add a layer of salt to 'em, too." He added the last with an emphatic nod. "I ain't given up whiskey, tobacco, nor women, neither. Even though that last one is gettin' harder and harder to find these days. I don't cotton to datin' young girls. I like 'em at least eighty."

They had a version of the same conversation every time Mel Helberger came in. Not because of faulty memories on either of their parts, but because of a shared camaraderie. Mel still had more than fifteen years on him, but Vern acknowledged the fact that he, himself, was hardly a young man.

He ran a keen eye over his patient, looking for tell-tale signs of poor health. His skin was pale, but the color had been steadily leaking out for the past twenty years. His clothes still hung loosely on his near-skeletal frame. Mel had never been a big man, but the years seemed to fuel themselves on whatever body fat he had accumulated. He showed no signs of unexplained weight loss or gain. No edema. No splotchy skin nor high color in his cheeks. Mel looked much the same as he had for the past fifteen or more years.

Perplexed, the doctor asked, "You feeling okay today, Mel?"

"I feel fine," he answered in a sharp voice.

He offered no other explanation for his presence, but Doc knew there was something more to it. Normally, Raley had to badger him into coming as often as every ninety days. Even the yearly exams had been unnecessary in Mel's opinion, but he relented if for no other reason than to drive the old '48 into town.

Waiting him out, Vern knew he would talk when he was ready. Poking his stethoscope in his ears, he leaned forward. "Since you're here, we might as well give you a once-over."

"Tryin' to earn your money, huh?" Mel grumbled.

"You know me, Mel. I'm nothing if not an honest man. No shenanigans on my watch."

He listened to the strong, steady pump reverberating in his ears. "Good, good," he murmured. "Give me a couple of deep breaths."

"I ain't gettin' up on that table," Mel warned him as the doctor looped the stethoscope back around his neck.

"Your knee hurting you again?"

"Ain't nothin' hurtin' me. I just don't wanna climb up on that table. Why dirty clean paper? We done kill enough trees as it is."

So. It was going to be one of those *days again*, the doctor thought to himself. Mel always had a cantankerous streak, but some days, he was grumpier than others. Today was obviously one of them.

"That's not a problem," Doc appeased him. "You don't have any stomach pain, do you?"

"Nope."

"Have you had any problems voiding your bladder?"

"If you mean am I peein', I ain't got no problem. Not with poopin', neither."

"Fine, fine. Then no need for the table," he assured him a second time. He eyed his patient again. "What about sleeping? Have you had any problems sleeping at night?"

"Nope. Other than the dreams, I sleep just fine."

That caught the doctor's attention. Mel Helberger was well-known for his dreams. Some went so far as to call him a seer. The future came to him in his sleep, they claimed. They said he was gifted with the sight.

"Dreams?"

"That's right."

Something about the way he said the words stirred the fine hairs at the back of Vern Dudley's neck. Almost with dread, the doctor lifted his eyes to meet the older man's gaze.

He shivered when he saw the look in them.

"What, uhm, what kind of dreams, Mel?" His

smooth demeanor slipped as a faint tremble crept into his voice.

"You know the kind, Doc." His voice was low. Heavy.

Vivid dreams were a well-known phenomenon for those nearing the end of their life's journey. Loved ones who had gone before them appeared in their dreams, as if welcoming them into the afterlife. The dreams were like a transition stage, offering the dying a sense of peace, knowing they would be reunited with old friends and beloved family members. It gave them courage to press toward the finish line, to think of death as a new beginning rather than the end.

It should come as no surprise that someone of Mel's age would have the same experience, but it shook the doctor just the same. He would miss his old friend.

"Anything you want to talk about, Mel?" he asked gently.

"I reckon that's why I'm here. I need to tell ya about my dream."

"I'm listening."

"I know what you're thinkin'. You think I had a dream about my Elva. About the boy we lost as a young 'un. About my favorite old hound Moody."

"All of those are perfectly normal, Mel. You and Elva had many happy years together, and I know you've been lonely since she passed. And no matter how long your son's been gone, I know you still mourn him."

"That ain't what I dreamed about."

"It wasn't?"

"No. It's worse than that."

The doctor kept his voice gentle. "Not all dreams are reassuring," he said with compassion. "Regrets tend to haunt us. Mistakes we made. Wrongs we should have made right. That's normal, too, Mel."

The other man drew back in disgust. "This weren't no death dream, Doc!" he objected. "Not about mine, no way."

"It wasn't?" Vern's brow crinkled with misunderstanding. "Perhaps you should tell me what your dream was about."

"Been more than one of them. I should have spoke up sooner, but I wasn't certain." He shifted uncomfortably in his chair. "Not until last night."

The statement piqued his curiosity. "What happened last night?" the doctor asked.

"I woke up in a cold sweat. Jolted me wide awake, just like it always does when it happens."

Despite the rumors surrounding Mel's gift, it was a topic the two of them had never broached before. Being a man of science, Doc had his doubts about clairvoyance. In his opinion, most seers were detail-orientated and naturally observant, picking up subliminal clues that often went unnoticed. While highly intuitive, he believed that people claiming to have the sight simply made educated guesses.

That said, it was an interesting subject. For his entire life, Vern had been surrounded by people who swore by the gift of sight. Area folklore practically demanded it. Tales had been handed down through the generations, embedding the firm belief that some people could see into the future. They were revered as wise and all-knowing.

More curious than convinced, the doctor asked, "When what happens?"

"When I know."

That weight was there again. It wasn't just the weight of his words. It was the weight of their meaning. There was something ominous in his old friend's voice.

Vern ran a hand over the back of his neck, willing the fine hairs back into place. He wasn't sure why he felt so nervous.

"What is it you think you know, Mel?"

"I don't think. I know."

He had never known his friend to be melodramatic. Mel was usually blunt to the point of being rude. With him, there was no beating around the bush. He whacked it off right where it stood, like it or not.

Vern respected his straight-forwardness, and he returned it in kind.

"Okay. What do you know?"

"You're in danger, Doc."

Stunned, for a moment Vern simply stared at him. It was an outlandish statement to make, yet he saw that his friend was quite sincere. "Danger?"

Mel stood by his claim. "That's what I said."

"What kind of danger? Like, I'm going to be in a car wreck?" He thought about last night, when he traversed the stairs to his basement with such care. He was serious when he asked, "Am I going to break my leg?"

"It's worse, Doc."

He thought of what happened later, when he dallied with one of the most upstanding ladies in the community. "Will I be ostracized for toying with a woman's affections? Will I—Will I lose my license for it?" He paled at the thought.

"No. You're going to be murdered."

The doctor struggled to regain his composure. "M-Murdered?"

"That's what I said."

"But... how? Who? Wh-Why?"

Mel shook his head. After ninety-nine years, he still had a full head of hair. The snowy white shock added color to his bleached-out face. "Don't got the answers or the why for," he said. "I just know the outcome. You, Doc, are about to meet your Maker. I thought I best warn you."

"Warn me from what?" Vern stood so quickly, the stool spun out from behind him. He threw his arms up in frustration. "How am I supposed to protect myself, if I don't know where the danger is coming from?"

"Not sure you can," Mel said bluntly. "But you can right them wrongs you were talkin' about. Get your affairs in order."

Vern's eyes narrowed. Was his old friend referring to physical affairs? Had some jealous husband or overprotective son put him up to this? Given his numerous female friendships, someone could be playing a sick joke on him.

"Did someone send you here today, Mel?" he asked suspiciously.

"'Course not!' he scoffed. "Who would be sending me?"

"That's what I asked you."

"Look. We go a long way back. I came here to warn

you on my own free will. I don't take orders from nobody."

"I didn't mean to offend you, Mel. I just... I don't know what to say about all of this."

"I don't reckon there's much you can say. Not to me, no how."

Vern paced the small room. He stopped long enough to look the old man in the eye. "Do you know... when?" His voice wavered with the question.

"I'd guess soon. Next few days, most likely."

The doctor was visibly shaken. He found the wayward stool and sat. Hard.

"I'm sorry to break it to you like this, Doc, but I thought you'd want to know."

His mouth worked, but no sound came out. He finally managed a strangled, "If I knew how... if I knew who..."

"Ain't got no answers for that."

The men sat in grave silence for several moments. Mel broke the silence with a question. "Can I do anything for ya, Doc? Get you anything?"

He wanted to lash out at the old man and tell him he had had quite enough for one day. He was responsible for this chunk of icy fear in his heart, for the hysteria taking over his lungs, and the mania swirling around in his head.

He said none of that. The old man meant well. "I don't... At this point, I don't know what I need."

Mel pushed to his feet. "Then I reckon I should be going." He stuck out his hand for a handshake. His grip was still firm and strong. "It's been a pleasure, Doc."

"I...you, too, Mel." Emotion clogged his throat, but

Vern pushed out the goodbye.

The old man stopped to look back when he reached the door. "If you got enemies, you might try to make peace with 'em. That might help."

Vern nodded faintly, murmuring some intelligible reply. For once, he didn't walk his patient to the front desk. He was lost in his own thoughts.

It was just a dream, he told himself. *People have them all the time. There's no need to overreact. Like I told Mel, surreal dreams are common as a person nears the end.*

Vern knew Mel wasn't just anyone. While he wasn't totally convinced the phenomenon was real, there were plenty of people who swore by Mel's uncanny predictions. The doctor couldn't shake the feeling that this time, Old Mel was right.

Mel had mentioned enemies, and Vern knew he had them. He could think of a hundred-thousand reasons one person, in particular, was his enemy. But there were others. He had been living on the edge for the last few years. He had become reckless and daring, and now it was coming back to haunt him.

The doctor kept a small flask in his desk drawer. Most days, it went untouched, but there were days when a small dose of reinforcement was appreciated. Today was definitely one of those days.

He uncapped the flask and took a swig of liquid strength. Another to soothe his nerves.

The third swig was for luck.

Vern closed his eyes. *Just a dream*, he told himself. *It was just a dream.*

9

The doctor slept poorly that night, a natural reaction after having one's death foretold. Ol' Mel may not have given him an exact date, but Vern had no doubt the prediction would come true. Everyone, of course, died at some point, but Mel's visions were known not only for their accuracy, but also for their timeliness. Vern doubted he would see the new moon crest.

He fell into a fitful sleep, thankful he didn't have to go into the office on Saturdays. He wasn't ready to face people just yet, knowing what he knew.

With the day looming before him, Vern went down to his basement. He saw no need to abandon his schedule simply because his death was somewhat imminent. He would make these last deliveries, if only to spare his children the worry of having illegal drugs in the house.

As he worked in the drying corner, turning the fresher product and removing those ready for harvesting, he thought of how his remaining days might play out. His ultimate fate was sealed, but he still had some options within his control.

Ironically, just as he found a way to meet his Wednesday deadline, his hopes for a prosperous future evaporated like dew under the hot sun. He would have the money from the trust by then. Even with the early withdrawal penalties and the assorted costs of restructuring his assets, there would be a generous payout. Combined with the advance from Hilda and their new business proposition, he should have no problem gathering the needed one-hundred-thousand dollars. If he came up a little short, he could beg for additional time.

At worst, Boss could order a hit and take the guesswork out of Mel 's prediction.

But there were other options.

He could simply ignore the debt and defy the loan shark. He would meet the same fate as the first option, but his children would still have their inheritance.

Alternately, he could try delaying the inevitable. Once he paid the debt and was no longer under Boss' thumb, it would be one less death threat to worry about. It seemed reasonable to assume that if he made peace with potential enemies who wished him dead, the same could be said for them. Rectifying the situation between them could buy him time and delay the timeliness of Mel's prediction. Right?

It was worth a try, so Vern pulled out some paper and started a list of those who had reason to kill him. There was no shortage of names to go on it. He would make amends right away, in hopes of extending his future. If it didn't work, he had nothing to lose.

There was, however, a third option. He had all this

product to be sold yet and, thanks to Hilda, a modest stash of cash in his home safe. Even if he had the money to repay Boss, what if he deliberately missed the meeting? Boss couldn't allow him to walk free—he had a reputation to uphold, after all—but he might not kill Vern immediately. He was just cruel enough to toy with a person and make them fear the unknown.

Vern, on the other hand, already knew he was going to die. If he couldn't appease all his enemies, his fate was sealed—everything but the date. Why not take his chances? Boss would kill him when he killed him. His children would still have their inheritance, (Catherine's status for additional funds was questionable) and Vern could enjoy his last days here on Earth, even if it were just seventy-two hours.

The more he considered it, the more certain he became. The third option made the most sense. He would make a few phone calls and set up appointments. He had a few clients in Missouri, but he dealt mostly in Oklahoma.

And while he was there selling the last of his supplies, he could hit the casinos one last time. Gambling was how he had gotten mixed up with Boss in the first place, but this time it would be different. For once, he could gamble worry-free, even if it meant losing it all.

Making a decision settled his nerves, and he was able to focus on his work.

Death was inevitable, and his was coming for him.

Let the chips fall where they may.

Vern worked all day getting more products ready. These weren't the salves and tinctures he made for patients. This was pure, quality weed, ready for recreational consumption. He had joints, blunts, dabs, and highly concentrated oils. Baggies with crushed and dried plants, ready for pipes, bongs, and vaporizing. This was the good stuff, pure and strong.

These were for the real money, and he was eager to get them into the hands of his best buyers.

He slept much better that night, knowing he had a plan. He would sell off everything he could—Hilda might not be happy, but he had never been quite honest with her about his inventory—let loose at the casinos, then come back and make what amends he could with his enemies.

He would call Lawrence and talk with his son one last time. He wished things hadn't ended as they had with Catherine, but she had made that choice. She was the one who had to live with it. Once he was cold and in the ground, it wouldn't bother Vern at all.

10

Something woke Willow in the night. She felt disoriented and slightly claustrophobic. Glancing at her bedside clock, she saw that it was 4:11 in the morning.

She lay still, listening. Had a noise shaken her from the grasp of slumber? Panic flashed through her, as her mind went back to the night someone bombed her car. The explosion had thrown debris against the brick and woke her. She sniffed the air now, searching for a whiff of smoke.

There was none. Nor was there a strange orange glow like there had been that night. But there was, even in the darkness, a sense of shadows. A feeling that something wasn't right.

Goosebumps stole across her, burrowing themselves beneath her skin. Something was wrong. Something was about to happen, and it wasn't good.

All hopes of falling back to sleep vanished. Willow knew she couldn't rest, not with this cloud of anticipation hanging over her. Resigned, she pushed back the covers and got out of bed.

As she started the espresso machine, she tried pinpointing the source of her unease.

There was no doubt she had concerns about the Fowler case. They weren't their typical clients. Truth be told, most of their clients hired them in opposition to people like the Fowlers. The Fowlers of this world were a rough lot. They tended to think that rules and laws didn't apply to them. They preferred taking things into their own hands and seeking their own brand of justice.

Rumor said there were bodies buried in Muskrat Holler. An old folk legend claimed Ezariah Fowler had gone crazy after losing all four sons to the War Between the States. He went on a killing spree, burying the bodies in a mass grave. People claimed it was the reason his crops grew so lush and full, when others around him failed. Years later, legend had it, a terrible flood came and washed the bodies down the mountainside. Afraid future crops would wither and die, the tale was that his descendants 'fed' the earth once a year with more bodies. Over the years, it became a ghost story, told around campfires and hikes in the woods. Eventually, it became a Halloween prank. Teenagers would sneak into the holler, trespassing on private property and sometimes damaging fall crops. It was no wonder the Fowlers protected what was theirs, but their methods were questionable. They began to play pranks of their own, the kind that involved real shotguns and real retaliation. They gained the reputation of being mean and dangerous. It did well in keeping trespassers away, but it did nothing for their social standing in the community. They became outcasts. As such, they retreated into their own world. A world where they made the laws, and they doled out justice.

Willow nor her mother and daughter were comfortable knowing the Fowlers dealt with illegal drugs. It was a far cry from dealing cocaine and opioids, but in the state of Arkansas, growing and selling marijuana was still against the law. There were certain medical exceptions, but those were highly regulated, with purchases allowed only through licensed dispensaries. Selling raw products straight from the farm was definitely illegal.

Was that why she still had goose pimples? Her scalp felt like there were ants crawling over it. Willow couldn't shake the feeling that something bad was about to happen. It woke her with such urgency, she was certain the danger was imminent.

She sifted through ideas, thinking of what could still go wrong with the Fowlers. She had avoided the horror of the rat mobile, but she had no doubt there were a host of other dangers that could befall this investigation.

So far, they had little luck finding the thief stealing from the Fowlers. Everleigh and Willow had staked out the farm three times now, and every vehicle had driven into and out of the farm at their appointed times. None of their employees or distributors had deviated off course.

Nor had any teenagers sneaked in, trying to score a little weed. No unauthorized vehicles had slipped in or slipped out. Unless someone had scaled the forty-foot cliffs surrounding the field and managed to get past the razor-wire fence, the road was the only access point to the fields. And according to the

Fowlers, the vehicles caught on surveillance video were all pre-authorized.

Willow measured, pressed, and extracted her espresso, working on autopilot. Her mind was busy spinning theories. There was always the chance that some of their employees weren't as trustworthy as the Fowlers believed them to be. The sons had expressed concern over a couple of the new hires, but Everleigh had done extensive background checks on them. Obviously, they had no qualms about working for an illegal operation, but they had clean records. There was no history of theft, arrests, or jail time. No ties to known growers or dealers. That wasn't to say they weren't dealing the product on their own or selling to more discreet sources, but there was no evidence suggesting such.

Willow hadn't dared to bring it up, but there was another possibility, and it hit much closer to home. No unauthorized vehicles came during surveillance, but the family had access to surveillance dates. If one of their own was stealing from the family coffers, they would know when to lay low. Most likely, the guards would never question their presence, no matter the hour.

"Accusing her own family," Willow said aloud, "is a sure way to make an enemy of Mama Fowler." She thought about it for a moment before shaking her head. "But, no, that's not it. It's something else."

"Maybe," she continued to reason, "their thief is the person in the little SUV. We never got a good look at it or the license plate number, but they said it was authorized. I guess it's one of their distributors, which explains why it came in the middle of the night."

Something stirred a memory. She recalled the look that had passed between Mama Fowler and Georgia. Mama Fowler instructed her daughter-in-law to give them the names of their scheduled distributors. Did that mean they had unscheduled delivery personnel? Someone who wasn't on their payroll but made occasional deliveries for them?

Was that where the danger came from? Was this the person cheating them? Could this unscheduled source be double-crossing the Fowlers somehow? Something more than just skimming profits?

Her mind went amok with ideas. Unbeknown to the Fowlers, it was a rival grower, determined to take out the competition. A supplier out to steal their clients. An angry customer, even an undercover agent, determined to expose their illegal operation.

The question became who, exactly, was in danger? The Fowlers? Or the other person?

Was that why they hired *Intuitive Investigations*? To find the guilty party and get revenge?

"Be honest, Willow. We all knew the Fowlers wanted some sort of retribution. They couldn't very well go to the police and report that someone was stealing from their illegal operation. We convinced ourselves they only wanted what was coming to them. They would collect the money and be satisfied. We told ourselves that, but only because we needed a way to justify taking the case. We knew their reputation. We knew they have tempers and a warped sense of justice. We knew, deep down, that they wouldn't just let this slide."

She poured steamed milk into her cup and asked

herself, "What now? Do we figure out the perpetrator, hand their name over to Mama Fowler, and let her sons decide the person's fate?" The thought didn't settle well on her stomach. "Or do we say we couldn't find anyone at fault—which, as of yet, we haven't— and that our job is done?" She doubted that thought would settle well on the Fowlers' stomachs.

Carrying the coffee to the couch, Willow continued her one-sided conversation. It was how she sorted out cases and made sense of them.

She thought of a new worry. "What if the thief finds out we're spying on them? That could definitely be dangerous. Is that why I have this feeling?"

Again, she discarded the idea.

"No, it's something else. Maybe it's not about the Fowler case at all. What if this feeling is something else?" She thought about her family. Would someone she cared about get hurt? She pictured them one by one, but her danger meter never moved. "It's still something else," she said with a shake of her head. "Have I done anything different these last few days? Is it someone I've encountered recently?" Like many dreams, sometimes the smallest event in real life could manifest itself into her subconscious. Sometimes those random incidents became one of her premonitions. It was one of the downfalls of being so highly intuitive and in tune with the environment around her.

"I know I haven't encountered Tobias lately," she muttered flippantly. "Not that he owes me an explanation. One coffee date and a couple of visits to Karnie doesn't obligate him to call me again, but would it kill him?"

Willow first met the former college professor at *Years Ago Antiques and Curiosities* while looking for a connection to a cold case they were working on. Twenty-five years ago, three college students had disappeared, never to be heard from again. She went in looking for a camcorder they left behind, not realizing the store owner had actually known the boys and taught them in one of his classes. With a personal stake in the outcome, he had helped Willow unravel the mystery. It took the help of Karnie, an old mountain woman known as a bone witcher, for them to discover their remains.

There had been an undeniable spark between them, but he was still mourning his late wife. In a way, Willow was still mourning the loss of her marriage. Not because she was still in love with Marcus, but because she was in love with the idea of happily ever after, and marriages that lasted through the ups and downs of life. Losing that had been a blow to everything she had ever believed in.

"Which is perfectly fine," she told herself. "I don't have time for a man in my life, anyway. Not Tobias, not Lane. Not anyone." Lane Jennings was a special agent for the US Marshal Service that she had worked with on a few occasions. They, too, shared a spark, but they had never explored it outside the work setting.

"Again, fine with me," she said. "But there's something I'm missing. This feeling isn't generic. It's too intense." Even now, she felt the shadows closing in around her. Something bad was about to happen. Something connected to her, no matter how vaguely.

She tried recalling something this week that didn't

revolve around the Fowler case. The only thing she could think of was stopping by the café in Gander.

The ants crawled down Willow's back.

"That's it!" The breath caught in her throat. "The man called Doc. The man called Pyle. The money, the Rocks. The deadline." The air thickened as she looked at the date on her watch. "Today is Wednesday! He has to pay up, or... or else!"

Who was the man? Should she find him and warn him?

"Warn him of what, Willow?" she demanded of herself. "He already knows he's in danger. He either has the money, or he doesn't. There's nothing I can do to stop it. Obviously, this Pyle man knows how and where to find him. I can warn him, but I can't protect him."

It was hardly a comforting thought, but it was true.

This man called Doc was on his own.

As of yet, the inevitable hadn't happened. No one had murdered him yet.

The doctor took little solace in the fact. Soon enough, Boss would rectify the matter. He would order Vern dead, and that would be that. His fate was sealed.

Vern had been living high for the past two days. Sales were better than expected. He had been wheeling and dealing, eager to make as much as he could. If he was going out, he planned to go out with his pockets full.

Even Lady Luck smiled down upon him. He was on

fire at the tables. And there were always beautiful women eager to keep him company. As long as he kept the drinks flowing and threw them some cash now and then, they clung to him like plastic wrap.

He was on a winning streak. A high far more potent than the stuff he peddled. But what goes up must come down, and down he came. His luck crashed and burned, and all the ladies, particularly Lady Luck, turned their backs on him.

Vern returned home to Missouri, his pockets far from full.

"Too much to think about," he muttered to himself. It was early, and he was still in his pajamas. Dawn hadn't yet streaked the skies with its gradually strengthening rays. "Particularly on an empty stomach."

Vern saw no reason to watch his cholesterol or sugar intake now. He had never been strict about it— he had too much of a sweet tooth for that—but he had set some guidelines for himself. He limited fried foods and eggs. He tried to never have more than two desserts in one day. And he seldom drank alcohol, except in social settings or during particularly stressful situations. This past week had more than qualified for the latter. He had probably consumed more alcohol in the last seven days than he had in the seven weeks prior.

"If my last meal comes today, I see no reason not to indulge," he reasoned.

With that mindset, he pulled all the leftovers from his refrigerator. They weren't breakfast foods, per se, and the combinations weren't typical. But today wasn't a typical day. It could very well be his last day on Earth. He might as well make it count.

He heated up the last of the potato medley from Erma, the smothered steak Helen dropped off, and warmed the berry pie from Lucille. It was already seven days old, but did it matter if it made him sick? He might very well be dead before the bacteria settled in his stomach. He arranged a plate of all the rest. The honey cake from Tilly, the new batch of cupcakes with edible petals and small berry-beads from Midge, Erma's rhubarb pie, and the mini strawberry pie dear Emmaline dropped off when he had to cancel last night's visit. He started not to add Paulette's walnut cookies, but they were decent enough when dipped in Tilly's special honey.

Vern couldn't eat it all, but he made a valiant attempt. A few bites of each one, with larger portions of those he liked best. He could die with a full stomach as easily as he could an empty one.

11

"I know it sounds crazy," Willow told her partners as their workday began, "but this is something I have to do. I have to go there and see for myself what happens."

"And get yourself killed in the process?" Arms crossed over her chest, Ireland clearly objected to her daughter's fool-hearty statement.

"I'll be careful. And I'll come up with some sort of plausible excuse for being there. I don't know what yet," she admitted, "but I'll think of something."

Ireland continued to glare at her. "Even if you pretend to be a tourist looking for Murder Rocks, they'll run you off. Most likely with guns!"

"I don't plan to be that stupid," Willow said with an indignant air. "I just want to see who shows up and, most importantly, who leaves."

"If you'd given me more time," Everleigh said with a frown, "I could have set up a camera to catch it all remotely. You wouldn't have to be anywhere near there to observe."

"I knew there was something shady about this

deal at the café, but to be honest, we've been so busy I forgot all about it. I woke up at four this morning with an eerie feeling. The shadows were all around me."

"That's because the sun wasn't up yet!" her mother huffed.

"You, of all people, know not to ignore our instincts. I often know when something bad's about to happen, the same way you try to change the outcome. It's in our DNA and can't be helped."

"If I thought I could change the outcome of this crazy idea of yours, believe me, I would!"

There was no use for further argument. Whether she admitted it or not, Ireland understood where her daughter was coming from. It was something she was compelled to do, and nothing would change her mind.

Willow turned toward Everleigh. "You really think it's too late for a camera?"

"I wouldn't want to risk being seen."

"Do you have any other ideas?"

Everleigh twisted her lips in thought. She brightened and started to say something. With a small shake of her head, she stopped herself. After another moment of thought, she came up with something.

"Can you still ride a bike?" she asked her mother.

"As in bicycle, or Harley?"

Everleigh hooted outright. "When did you ever ride a Harley?"

Scrunching her nose, Willow couldn't deny her daughter's incredulous response. "Bicycle, it is. And it's been a while, but I guess so. They say it's something you never forget."

"Doesn't mean it's something you can always do. It

requires balance.”

“So far, so good.”

“In that case, I have an idea.”

“Great. What is it?”

“We can rent a couple of bikes and pretend to be out riding. It gives us a chance to go by at least twice. And if we have bike problems nearby…” She shrugged and lifted her palms upright in an innocent gesture.

“That might work. If I can manage the hills and the curves,” Willow mumbled.

“All the better reason for us to go slow. And we’d probably need a rest stop, too.”

“Maybe in a graveled parking area?” Willow suggested, a playful grin lighting her face.

“Exactly. Road safety and all that.”

“You two are impossible!” Ireland said, throwing her arms up in frustration.

“It’s the perfect cover, Landee. Not as many people ride the state and connecting highways,” Everleigh pointed out.

“If I recall, the road is too narrow for decent shoulders. You’d have to ride on the actual highway.”

Willow frowned. “We have enough sense to move when a car is coming, thank you very much.”

“Where are you getting these bicycles?”

“They rent them for day rides all the time,” Everleigh said. “I’ll look up rental places right now.”

“For the record, I still think this is a terrible idea.”

“Noted,” Willow said. “But it’s something I have to do.”

Instead of renting bikes for the day, Everleigh’s

friend Robin had two she volunteered to loan them. Not only that, she offered to take them to a drop-off spot about three-quarters of a mile from their destination. Her eyes burned with curiosity, but she didn't press when Everleigh said it was for a case and that she wasn't at liberty to say more.

It had been years since Willow had been on a bicycle, so it took a few minutes for her to get in the groove again. Once she mastered the balancing act, she was good to go.

"I'm not as worried about this Pyle guy," she confided to her daughter as they started out, "as I am passing out from oxygen deprivation. I'm already having trouble breathing. Guess I'm more out of shape than I realized."

"I *knew* I was!" Everleigh said candidly.

"New plan. We take a break before we get within sight of the area, and another one the minute we get out of sight. That's plus the one at the trail head."

"I like it."

They rode on, tackling curves and hills as they came. On an easy downward slope, Everleigh asked, "What, exactly, are we hoping to accomplish?"

It took a moment for Willow to answer. She wasn't sure she quite understood it herself, but she felt compelled to come.

"I guess I want to see for myself if the doctor came up with the money. After this morning, I'm guessing he didn't. Something bad is going to happen. Considering the fact I don't know the doctor and don't know the threat, I can't stop it, but...but maybe I could make it better."

"How? If the man is in that deep, what can you

possibly do to help? Aside from a loan, that is."

"As if! But maybe I could be there to comfort him. If they… I mean, if he's out there alone, and… hurt, we could at least call for help." It was hard to articulate what she was feeling. She knew it was worse than a few broken bones. The doctor's life was in danger.

"What if this Pyle guy is still in there? We can't afford for them to get suspicious of why you and I are there."

"It's a public highway. We have every right to ride our bikes on it."

Everleigh looked around. There were no vehicles in sight. In fact, they had only passed one so far. "I'm starting to agree with Landee. Maybe this wasn't the best idea. I didn't realize how exposed I would feel on a bike. At least with a car, you can duck down and hide. And hopefully outrun anyone chasing you. But on a bicycle…"

"If you want to go back, I don't blame you. You don't have to do this with me."

"There's no way I'd leave you out here on your own!"

"But if you want to—"

"I don't."

After a few more minutes and another incline, Willow was huffing and puffing. "How much farther is it?"

Everleigh consulted her GPS. "Uhm, we haven't gone very far. It's still over a quarter mile."

"You're kidding me."

"Want to stop?"

"Yes, but we can't afford to waste time."

"I wonder which way he'll come from? We haven't

seen many cars out here."

"I know." The chills were back, even though she was starting to sweat with exertion. It wasn't a good sign. Even worse were the hazy shadows she felt creeping in.

They rode on, until Everleigh gave her the blessed news. "It's just up there."

"Thank the Lord!" Willow gladly stopped peddling and glided to a stop. She pulled out her water bottle and chugged a greedy few sips.

"Go easy on that," Everleigh warned. While hardly an experienced cyclist, she and Laura Beth sometimes rode together.

"I know. I just didn't realize how out of shape I was!" Using the neck of her shirt, she mopped up the sheen of sweat gathering at her throat. "Wow. That was tough on an old woman."

"We aren't even there yet. Plus, we have to go past it, and then back again."

"I vote we call Lucy to pick us up the minute we're back to this spot."

Everleigh laughed. "It's not that bad. Rest another minute or two, then let's go on. Remember, they don't know how far we've already come. Our stopping point could be just past the Rocks."

"Second that."

They pulled back on the road and peddled on. They came to the parking area, but a dark-blue Chevy truck was the only vehicle there. By mutual accord, they rode on.

"The actual Murder Rocks," Everleigh said in a low voice that wouldn't carry, "are closer to that curve up there. Maybe we could have bike trouble there."

The rocks weren't visible from the road but, over time, foot traffic left a faint trail through the woods. The two women completed the curve, turned their bicycles around, and started back in the opposite direction.

Only the fence and a pocket of wooded terrain separated them from the famed location. Once upon a time, long before the paved highway was built, the Springfield-Harrison Road was a dirt passage cutting through these very woods. As a major thoroughfare for the area, it served stagecoaches, wagons, and, unfortunately, outlaws like Alf Bolin and his gang. The outlaws would hide behind the elephant-shaped rocks and ambush unsuspecting travelers, relieving them of their valuables. Sometimes, their victims lost more than their pocket watches, reticules, and gold coins; the most unfortunate of travelers lost their lives. Folks started referring to the large limestone outcropping as Murder Rocks.

Willow hoped the boulders didn't live up to their name again today. What was to say that even if the doctor did pay his debt, this Pyle guy didn't kill him anyway? That would definitely explain the darkness she sensed.

"I'm going closer," Willow whispered to her daughter.

"Are you crazy?" her daughter replied emphatically.

"Maybe. But I'm also curious. And worried."

"So am I, now that you're stopping your bike!" Everleigh hissed.

"You can stay, but I'm going in."

Everleigh knew arguing was useless. She followed

her mother's lead. They stashed their bikes near the makeshift trail, laying them on their sides so they weren't easily seen. Soon, they were on the other side of the fence, trespassing on private property. If caught by the landowner or law enforcement, they would chalk it up to ignorance.

They stopped to listen, straining their ears for movement ahead. Unsure of how far they were from the site, Willow moved carefully forward. Following instinct more than anything, she led their stealthy approach.

It was a slow process. They watched where they stepped, avoiding sticks that could snap and obstacles that could hinder. When they finally saw the rocks through the trees, they stopped. Without a word to the other, Willow and Everleigh pressed themselves against a tree and listened. There were no voices. No sounds of movement.

Everleigh looked at her mother with a question in her eyes. Willow replied with a shrug. After waiting a few moments more, she motioned forward and took a tentative step. When no one jumped out from behind a nearby tree, she took another step, then another.

Slowly and almost silently, they were within feet of the rocks. Still no sounds of life, which worried Willow even more. A glance at her watch told her it was twelve after two.

She had no doubt that Pyle meant two o'clock. She recalled his words at the diner. 'Not one minute after,' he had said. That meant she had either missed the man called Doc, he hadn't shown up, or that she was too late. He had already met his fate.

Instinct told her it was the latter. She crouched

low and moved closer, ignoring Everleigh's attempt to hold her back.

When Everleigh stepped on a tiny stick, the snap sounded deafening to their ears. They were out in the open, with no place to hide without diving for cover. If anyone was out here, they would definitely be caught.

Again, no one came from the other side of the rocks. They released the air pooled in their lungs as quietly as possible. Steadying their nerves, they crept closer. The air felt heavier the closer they came to the rocks. It was early afternoon, and even though they were among shadows cast by the trees and budding leaves overhead, Willow felt the darkness. The sensation was so strong, it was almost visible. Was the doctor on the other side of the rocky formation, already shot through the heart? Did his blood seep into the soil? She couldn't have missed him by more than a few minutes. Would it have mattered, or would she have risked her own life—and, more importantly, her daughter's—in vain?

Having reached the rocks, Willow put her hand out to keep herself steady. The ground around the large formation was littered with smaller rocks, and she didn't want to stumble. If someone was on the other side, she wanted to peek around without being seen rather than announce her presence with a cry of pain.

Everleigh allowed a few feet between them. If her mother pulled back, she didn't want to be in the way. The less fumbling, the better.

The moment Everleigh touched the rock, she felt a jolt of horror. She didn't know if it was from present danger or the many past transgressions that had taken place here. These rocks were soaked in blood, as surely as if they were painted red. While not visible to the eye, the scars of evil crippled her heart. She almost staggered beneath the pain. Scenes flashed before her eyes. Microseconds of faces she didn't know, horrified eyes she had never seen, expressions that turned her blood cold. Everleigh experienced the same terror of knowing your life was ending, just as these poor souls had.

Tears streamed down her face as she jerked her hand away. Only a few seconds had passed, but she had experienced the devastation of decades in that time. It lingered still, and she knew the bloodshed hadn't ended with the Bolin Gang. There had been suicides here, a terminal man who came here to die, and yes, more murders. She didn't know the details, but she was certain of the fact.

Everleigh brushed away the tears to keep her eyes clear and alert for danger. Snails moved faster than her mother did, but eventually Willow disappeared around the rock. Knowing it was safe to follow, Everleigh moved just as silently. Her pace wasn't quite as slow.

They cleared the first massive rock and started around the second. They froze when they heard rustling nearby. Someone was stomping over the leaves, snapping branches, and making no effort to be stealthy.

"Keep your head down," Willow hissed.

They heard a man's voice. Like that day in the café, she couldn't see a face. She wouldn't risk their position by poking her head around the rock. From the sound of it, the man was on the phone, and he was angry. "I'm telling you, the fool didn't show!"

It sounded like he was pacing. His footsteps waned and waxed. The question was how close would he come? Would he eventually see them there, huddled behind Murder Rocks?

Willow and Everleigh both had their guns. The firearms were safely holstered, and unless they risked making a sound to pull them out, they did no good. Even so, were either of them brave enough—or foolish enough—to replay history and ambush the man on the other side?

"I don't know!" the man yelled into the phone. "I'm telling you, he didn't show. I don't know where he is!"

The last words were fainter, as if he were going away from them. Willow looked at Everleigh and motioned to the woods, her fingers making the universal walking sign. Everleigh shook her head, but Willow's hand gestures became more adamant. She indicated for the younger woman to go first, and she would follow.

Everleigh still looked uncertain. The woods directly behind them were denser than the ones they had come through. *Like, by five trees.* The bitter thought ran through her mind as she calculated their chances. If they could sneak into the woods without him seeing, they could go deep enough in and circle back to the road. As long as he didn't see them going for the bikes, they could make a clean getaway.

If, if, if. Their life depended on ifs.

Another prompt from her mother, and Everleigh made her move. She aimed for the biggest tree she saw and slipped behind it.

The man's voice grew stronger again, but she couldn't hear his words over the loud thumping in her chest. Still crouched behind the rock, Willow's eyes were glued ahead, but she held a 'hold on a sec' finger toward her daughter.

It seemed like an eon, but Willow finally hurried over, her back still hunched at the waist. One by one, they retreated to the next big tree.

"Hey! Who's there?" the man called out. Crunched leaves testified to him coming closer. "Is someone there?"

They risked another tree.

"I'll call you back." He spoke brusquely into the phone. Neither woman dared peek, but they imagined him pocketing his phone and reaching for his gun.

Freeing their own firearms, Willow and Everleigh were on high alert. Two of them, one of him. Other than the fact that neither of them had ever shot another human being, the odds were in their favor.

"Is someone out there?" the man called again. His voice came closer. "Doc? Is that you? If it is, you're late."

Their slow, methodic pace hadn't carried them far. Moving much faster, the man would be upon them soon.

Everleigh tapped her mother's shoulder to get her attention. Then she bent and picked up a rock. She tested its weight in her hand. *Good enough*, she decided. She threw it as far and hard as she could.

It landed far to their left, making a solid thud as it collided with a tree. For added sound effects, it bounced off the tree and landed on a rotted limb. It cracked, and the man fired.

As the gunshot echoed through the woods, Everleigh and Willow took their chance. There was no time to step carefully. No time to move quietly. They ran as fast as they could, angling toward the highway, knowing they sounded like a bear crashing through the woods.

A second shot hit the ground behind them. A third splintered a tree to their left.

Without taking time to look back, Willow aimed her gun behind them and pulled the trigger. She was almost relieved when he shot back. At least she hadn't made an as-luck-would-have-it kill shot.

They were getting close to the road. A vehicle had finally come along, and they heard its motor just through the woods. If they could make it to the road…

And what? Willow asked herself. What would they do then? Unless they could flag it or another vehicle down, they would have exposed themselves in a wide-open space. The man in the woods could pick them off like the sitting ducks they would be.

Another shot, this one closer, and she knew it was worth the risk. Surely, there was a house somewhere near here.

Everleigh was one step ahead. While Willow contemplated their chances, her daughter was already on the phone. "Robin! Come get us! No time to explain but call the police! We're on the other side of the parking area, not sure how much. And yes, that was a gunshot you heard. Hurry!"

The shot was closer to them now, suggesting the shooter was, too. Willow fired again.

"There's the fence!" Everleigh heaved, out of breath from the harried pace and, in no short amount, from fear. "I'll cover you while you crawl through."

"No! You go first."

"Too late," Everleigh said. She was already firing her gun.

Willow heard her shirt rip as she crawled under the barbed wire, but it was the least of her worries. Everleigh and the man exchanged another round of fire before she made it through.

"Your turn," Willow said, taking over the defensive action. She fired into the woods as Everleigh chose to crawl through two strands of wire. Not only did her shirt rip but also one leg of her pants. As the material snagged, she fell unceremoniously to the ground. She was up before her mother had time to bend over her.

"No time," she said, even though her skin was ripped, as well. "Let's go!"

"Do you see that car we heard?" Willow asked. It had been going in the direction opposite their bikes, not that it mattered.

"No. But I see a truck coming. Let's flag them down."

"With guns in our hands?" She knew it was useless, but she wasn't ready to tuck it away yet. Not with the man still in the woods.

It was their best hope but impossible. No sane person would stop to pick up two women brandishing guns.

Now what do we do?

12

Everleigh let out a relieved whoop. "Calvary to the rescue! That's Tobias hanging out the window."

Willow had a ton of questions, but they could wait. She pushed Everleigh forward so that she had her back. She still held her pistol, ready to fire if necessary.

"Hurry!" Tobias said needlessly. "Get in!"

He had reached across the truck to open the passenger side door. Everleigh scrambled inside, sitting lopsided between the seat and the console. Comfort was the least of her concern. The moment Willow's feet were inside, Tobias Cameron gunned the engine. She closed the door as they sped down the highway.

"What are *you* doing here?" Willow demanded, looking over her daughter to glare at him.

"Shh," Everleigh said, already dialing her phone. "I gotta call—Robin? Don't come. We caught a ride, and I don't want you anywhere near here…. Yes, I'm sure. Look, I'll call you later. Just, please, stay away. And I'll replace your bikes, I promise."

"No need," Tobias interrupted. "They're in the back."

"Never mind," Everleigh corrected. "I'll call you soon. Thank you for everything, and stay away from here, okay?" She hung up before her friend could ask questions, including how to explain her 9-1-1 call.

"That's done, so what are you doing here?" Willow demanded a second time.

"Apparently, saving your hide." Hearing her ungrateful response to his presence, she saw a nerve working along the jawline his goatee didn't cover.

"I'm not some damsel in distress!" she protested.

Everleigh, sitting a bit higher than her because of the console, looked down with a smirk. "You kinda are right now," she reminded her mother. "We both are."

Ignoring the logic, Willow's stance didn't soften. "How did you know to come?"

"Your mother called."

"Of course she did," Willow muttered darkly.

"Branson isn't that far away. I could be here faster than she could."

"But she has Laura Beth!" Everleigh squealed.

"Which is why she didn't come. She did the next best thing, which was to call me. Even," he said, throwing Willow a look, "if your mother can't appreciate that."

"The police would have been the better choice," Willow said.

"Really? You were trespassing on private land, even though people do it all the time. And from what I heard, you were firing a weapon. A weapon you're holding while riding down the road, which is also illegal."

Willow looked down at her pistol as if just noticing it. She hastily stuffed it back in its holster.

"You heard the shots?" Everleigh asked.

"Yeah. Your grandmother told me where you were. I was just getting out of the truck when I heard gunshots. They sounded close to the road, so I took a chance. I saw your bikes, put them in the truck, and heard more shooting. I saw you coming out of the woods and came to pick you up," he explained. He kept looking behind in the rearview mirror. So far, there was no sign of the blue truck following them.

"So, I guess you saw my graceful fall." Everleigh's voice was sardonic, but when she put her hand down to her leg, it came away with blood.

"You're bleeding! You weren't hit, were you?" Willow frantically tried to see the wound, but it was on the inside of her leg.

"Only by a sharp barb," she admitted. "And, yeah, my pride took a licking, especially since there was a witness."

"I'm just glad I got there in time," Tobias assured her. "Are you two okay?"

"Winded," was all Willow would admit to.

"From both exertion *and* fear," Everleigh expounded on her mother's brief answer. She looked down and frowned at her, not understanding the hostile attitude any more than Tobias did.

"What were you two thinking, anyway?" he barked at them.

"Hold the criticism, will ya?" Everleigh asked. "And don't look at my big butt as I crawl over this console. This isn't exactly comfortable, you know."

"I'm sorry I can't stop, but just in case the truck is behind us…"

Willow hadn't thought to worry about that. No matter how in control she tried to sound, her nerves were still a tangled mess.

"And," he added, "it's easier to go in at an angle, head first. Lean behind my seat and just slide in."

"And kick my mother in the head?"

"Maybe it will knock some sense into her," he muttered under his breath.

"I heard that!"

Everleigh ignored them both. "Okay. Here goes."

The process was even less graceful than her fall beside the fence, but after several fumbles, kicking the dashboard several times and her mother once, Everleigh managed to slide into the backseat's floorboard.

"You okay?" Willow asked when she just lay there.

"Just resting," the redhead assured her. "Whew! That wasn't easy." She hauled herself up and eased into the seat. By now, the blood had soaked through her ripped jeans.

"Do you need to go to the doctor? That's a lot of blood," her mother said in alarm.

"Just because my heart is pumping overtime. Let me just lie here a minute and rest."

"There should be a towel in the seat," Tobias said, looking at her through the mirror. "Press it between your legs to staunch the flow. If it soaks through, we're going to the ER."

"Prop it up, too. Get it higher than your heart," Willow advised. "Use that tool bag."

"Gym bag," Tobias corrected.

She glanced over at him. Of course he worked out. He had the body to prove it.

"And don't worry. The towel is clean," he offered the information. "There's another in my bag if you need it."

Everleigh would never admit it, but she was in too much pain to even consider whether or not the towel was clean. "And I liked these pants," she mumbled.

Turning his gaze on Willow, he used his 'professor voice.' "Now," he said in a no-nonsense approach, "you were telling me why the two of you were in those woods."

"I was?"

"Don't play innocent. Why were you there?"

"Being a professor and teaching local history as you did, I'm sure you're aware of the significance of Murder Rocks. We wanted to see them for ourselves."

"The least you can do is be straight with me. Your mother already told me you were there on some cockamamie idea—her words, not mine—and that you wouldn't listen to reason. I came because she was genuinely worried about the two of you. She suspected you'd do something foolish, like go in for a closer look."

"Oh, my word! I need to call her! I can't believe I haven't yet." Willow's flustered frustration was sincere. Tobias made no move to stop her as she pulled out her phone and hit speed dial.

"We're okay," was the first thing off her tongue. "Seriously. I don't know why you called for backup, but we're fine."

Ireland's fiery protest was hard to miss. When Willow couldn't get a word of her own in, Tobias took the phone from her hands. "Ireland?" he said, interrupting the older woman's tirade. "I'm sorry to cut this short. They really are fine, but Lucy has some s'plaining to do." He mimicked Ricky Ricardo's most famous line.

He punched 'end' and handed the phone back to her.

"How dare you!" she fumed.

"I dare, because you just exchanged gunfire with someone in the middle of nowhere. What were you thinking, Willow? You're lucky Everleigh was only hit by a fence, not a bullet!"

The implied accusation cut her short. He was right. Everleigh could have been killed. She looked over the seat. "You okay, honey? How are you feeling?"

"Too tired to complain," she replied.

"Why don't you try to take a nap?"

"With all that yelling up there?"

"We're not yelling."

"I can feel the hostility between you two all the way back here. What's that all about, anyway?"

Willow rolled her eyes and mumbled, "You're the empath."

"You're right. I am. How's this for reading the room? Or, truck," she amended. "Tobias doesn't understand what he did wrong. He came to help, and you jumped down his throat."

The woman was good. "What she said," their driver grunted.

"And you're angry because he came to rescue you, and you're trying to be an independent woman and hate to admit how scared we both were out there."

"Whose side are you on?" Willow protested.

"Careful, or I'll throw in the part about you being mad because he hasn't called."

"Everleigh!" Willow's face was already aflame.

Tobias didn't reply. He was busy watching the rearview mirror. Seeing his frown, Willow turned to look back.

"What is it?" she asked in alarm. "What do you see?"

"There's a dark pickup behind us. It looks like it's blue, but I can't tell for sure. They're keeping their distance."

"Tailing us," Willow acknowledged. It was the cornerstone of successful surveillance. Keep the subject in sight without creating suspicion.

"There's a road up here. It's a windy road that eventually leads back toward Border. Do either of you get carsick easily?"

Willow shook her head.

From the backseat, Everleigh gave an honest answer. "Not usually, but today I make no promises."

"If you need to have that stitched up," the former professor said decisively, "we'll go straight into Branson."

"I think the bleeding has stopped, but the hurting continues." She tried making light of the situation.

"Are you sure?" Willow asked in concern.

"Mind over matter, right?"

"Maybe you can sleep on the way home?"

"I'll try."

Tobias checked the mirror again. "The turn is right past the curve. Hold on to something. It's going to get rough."

He didn't hit the brakes. He couldn't risk the other driver seeing his taillights. He let off the gas instead, but they were traveling fast enough that it made little difference. Tobias fought for control of the truck as he whipped it sharply to the right. Willow bit back a scream as the truck fishtailed and headed toward a tree. Everleigh slid off the seat, hitting the floorboard with a thud.

She cried out in surprise but managed to reassure them, "I'm okay, I'm okay."

His jaw clenched tight, Tobias had a death hold on the steering wheel. He couldn't afford to reply. He couldn't worry about their discomfort or their muffled cries. His only concern was to keep his wheels on the road and not in the ditch. Hitting the brakes now would put them in a tailspin. He had to keep going, his foot still off the gas. Momentum still pushed them forward.

"Check the mirror," he told Willow. "See if he followed."

She turned backward in her seat. "I don't see him." It was promising, but not definitive. "Oh!' she said excitedly. "There he goes! It worked! He just went by."

Tobias blew out a breath. His hands still gripped the wheel, his knuckles white. "Sorry, but we can't afford to slow down," he told his harried passengers. "Sooner or later, he'll realize we turned off. If he knows the area, he knows where this road leads. He'll either turn around or try to intercept us."

"Intercept?"

"I told you it's a winding road. There's a series of intersecting roads."

Everleigh moaned from her place on the floorboard. "Is it safe to get up now? I don't want to go flying off the seat again." His gym bag rested upon her back, along with a jacket and a box that had been beside it. Its contents were now scattered all over the floor beside her.

Tobias took his eyes off the road just long enough to glance back at her. "I'm sorry, Everleigh. I had to cut it sharp, but that should be the worst of it."

She hauled herself up on the seat for the second time, taking the gym bag and jacket with her. Propping her leg up on the bag again, she turned herself sideways to get comfortable and secured her seatbelt. She bunched the jacket up to put behind her head.

"I should have taken the helmet Robin offered," Everleigh grumbled.

It was a long ride back to the main highway, no matter how fast Tobias drove. After dozens of curves and several turns, whizzing through farmland and tiny communities she had never heard of, Willow was thoroughly turned around.

"How do you know all these roads?" she asked in amazement. "This is like a maze!"

"I taught Ozark history, remember? Traci and I were notorious for impromptu road trips, chasing down historical sites and rumored legends. Sometimes they were for the store, finding estate sales and out of the way bargains. I've traveled many a back roads in the Ozark Mountains."

Buying the antique shop from Tobias' parents had been Traci's dream, not his. But when she died three years ago, he had kept her dream alive. Now, he was as passionate about antiques as he was in other aspects of history.

"I just hope Pyle doesn't know them," she grunted.

"We've passed the road I was most worried about," he assured her. "After that, it splinters so many times, it would be sheer luck if he found us."

"I noticed you slowed down a mile or two." The scenery still passed with a blur, and she kept her hand on the grab bar. In the back, Everleigh attempted to sleep, grunting with every bump and each sweeping curve.

"You know the guy who was shooting at you?" Tobias asked.

"Just his name."

"Your mom was sketchy with the details. Why don't you color it in for me?"

Willow hesitated before answering. So far, they had danced around the subject of her special gift. He knew she had the innate but unexplainable ability to *know* things, yet they had never fully discussed it. She dreaded when that day came; not everyone understood, or believed it was real.

Today wouldn't be that day.

"If you must know, I overheard a conversation a week ago. A man named Pyle wanted another man to meet him here at 2:00 to... conduct business." It seemed like the easiest way to describe the ultimatum. "I thought it sounded sketchy—different meaning of your word—so we decided to ride our bikes out here and see what was going on." She shrugged as if it were no big deal.

"Except they weren't your bikes, and your mother said it was dangerous. What kind of 'business' was this they were conducting?"

"I honestly don't know."

"Yet you felt compelled to come."

"Exactly."

"Willow. What aren't you telling me? And before you act like it was nothing, let me remind you that this man was shooting at you. And you were shooting back. I'm pretty sure you don't just go around shooting at people in the woods. You had to have a reason."

"I did. He was shooting at us. I was defending myself and my daughter. And I never shot *at* him. I was shooting to cover our backs."

"Real bullets, Willow. Real danger. Tell me why."

She wanted to say she was working a case, but it would be a lie.

"I deserve to know," Tobias pushed. "I put myself at risk to make sure the two of you were all right."

It was a low blow, but true. With a heavy sigh, she admitted, "I don't know the nature of their business, but I do know it wasn't on the up and up. This Doc owed money to Pyle's boss, and he planned to collect."

"How much?"

Willow winced as she spoke. "A hundred thousand."

"*Dollars*? They were conducting a one-hundred-thousand dollar-deal in the woods, and you poked your nose into it?" Tobias was incredulous. "Are you insane?"

From the backseat, Everleigh never opened an eye. She reminded them to tone it down with one word. "Yelling."

"Seriously, Willow!" he said, his voice only slightly lower. "What were you thinking?"

"That maybe I could help? I was afraid Doc was in danger. I don't know him, don't even know his name, but we had a pleasant exchange after Pyle left. He seemed like a perfectly nice man who had gotten in over his head."

"So, why didn't you call the sheriff's office?"

"Honestly? It never crossed my mind."

Tobias smacked the steering wheel with his fist. This was a side of him she had never seen. She had seen him sad. Riddled with unnecessary guilt. Angry with the cruel fate those boys were dealt. But those emotions were justified. He had every right to be angry with what happened to his former students.

This anger was different. She didn't understand why he was so upset with her. Yes, she had done something stupid. Things were always more obvious in hindsight. And yes, she had been less than appreciative when he showed up. She should be angry with her mother, not him.

"I'm sorry I didn't thank you for coming to get us, Tobias." Her voice was contrite. "I had no idea the man would see us. He wasn't there when we went in, but he must have turned around and come back. We heard him on the phone, telling someone that Doc never showed up. We tried to sneak away, but a twig snapped, and he heard us. He just started shooting at us. It was the adrenaline. The shock. The fright. I—I just snapped at you, and I'm sorry."

They were coming into another town, this one larger than the others. There was a certain feeling of safety among others, no matter how misguided the feeling might be. Tobias relaxed enough to loosen his death grip on the wheel.

Stroking his neatly trimmed goatee, he accepted her apology. "I came down pretty hard on you, too. I guess I was scared for the two of you, and I know your mom was." He looked in the rearview mirror. "Everleigh? There's an Urgent Care Clinic up ahead. Do you need to go?"

"Thanks, but I'm good."

"I'll ask Landee to bring Laura Beth to my house. You can spend the night with me tonight." It wasn't much of an invitation. As far as Willow was concerned, it was settled.

"That's not necessary," Everleigh said, but the protest was weak.

"I'd feel better about you being there. In case you start hurting more in the night, I'll be there to help. If nothing else, I can get Laura Beth off to school, and you can sleep in."

Everleigh just nodded, a sure sign that her feisty daughter was in more pain than she let on.

"You don't mind taking us there, do you?" Willow thought to ask Tobias.

"Not at all. I assumed that's where we were headed."

"Thanks. I'd better call Landee and let her know."

<h1 style="text-align:center">13</h1>

It was rare for Dr. Vern Dudley to take a day off. He loved his job and the patients he cared for. He had called in sick two days that week, claiming to have a stomach bug. But when the doctor didn't call nor show up on Wednesday—again, so foreign to his customary behavior—Raley Bumgartner went to his house. She knew where he kept his spare key, as did most people in their small town. Crime was so rare, half the citizens didn't even bother locking their doors.

She stepped into the kitchen and called his name.

There was no answer, so she called out again.

She found him on the sofa, already cold. There was a plate of half-eaten sweets on the coffee table, and most of his stomach contents spilled across his chest and onto the floor. Raley turned hastily away, lest she lose her own breakfast. She called 9-1-1 and hovered by the door, outside, until the police came.

Without thinking, Raley called the office and gave them the horrible news. Myrtle Newton, another of the receptionists, was so stunned, she unwittingly blurted it out to the entire waiting room.

"What? Dr. Dudley is *dead*? … Right there in his living room? … Oh, Sweet Jesus! This is unbelievable!"

Cries of disbelief echoed around the room and down the hall. All around the clinic, cell phones came alive as people rushed to tell their friends. News of Vern Dudley's death spread like wildfire. By the time the authorities were able to reach the doctor's children and give them the heartbreaking news, half the county already knew.

Among the first to know were the members of the Spring Fling planning committee. With the celebration just one week away, they met more often to ensure that this year's event was successful. At least four phones rang simultaneously, with the others ringing just moments later.

Lucille Gardner was so upset, she excused herself to rush home, where she could grieve in private. She got as far as her car before breaking down in sobs.

As a group, they held hands and said a prayer. They pulled apart, mingling among themselves with murmurs of disbelief and conjecture. Whispers and rumors abounded.

Tilly Orbach, Emmaline Freely, Justine Paul, and Paulette Weeks hid tears and sniffles behind their tissues, discreetly shooting each other furtive glances.

Did the others know? They all wondered.

Tilly wasn't the only one with a secret. None of theirs were a matter of life or death.

But all of them were close enough.

As the county's acting coroner, Dr. Dudley's death presented a problem. Rather than sending his body off for a formal autopsy, a ruling of death from natural causes was decided by his peers and the sheriff's office. Heart attack, they assumed, was the most likely culprit.

His son wanted to have the service at the church his family had always attended. Catherine was content to have it at the funeral home. But the outcry of sympathy, support, and heartfelt concern demanded a larger venue.

Ultimately, the service was held in the school gymnasium. The air was thick and cloying from the scores of pot plants and floral arrangements overflowing from the stage. As was customary in the South, friends brought food for the bereaved, and a meal was served after the service. To seat everyone, the meal was also held at the school. The cheese-laden casseroles and decadent desserts—many of them the doctor's favorites, prepared just the way he liked them—were far superior to anything normally served in the cafeteria.

The whole town was in mourning, and half the county.

Vern Dudley had been a well-loved man.

And the day after his funeral, Lawrence Dudley began looking for answers behind his death.

"Our ten o'clock should be here soon," Everleigh reminded her partners.

"Are you sure you feel like working today?" Ireland worried. "We can handle this if you don't."

"I'm fine. The infection is almost gone, and my leg is just sore now."

"If you're sure…" Willow, too, was concerned about the youngest of their trio. That barbed wire had left her with a ragged scar and a nasty infection.

"I am."

"Remind me of his name. Lawrence, wasn't it?"

"Yes. Lawrence Dudley."

Two minutes later, the bell above the front door jingled, and a distinguished-looking man in suit and tie stepped through. A head full of salt-and-pepper hair suggested he was in his late forties to early fifties. The solemn set of his face and his red-rimmed eyes suggested he was having a rough day.

Everleigh's smile was warm and encouraging. "Welcome to *Intuitive Investigations*. You must be Mr. Dudley."

"That's right. Please, call me Lawrence." When he smiled, it eased the stress lines around his mouth and eyes.

"It's nice to meet you. I'm Everleigh, and these are my partners, Willow and Ireland."

He had a nice, firm handshake, even if his eyes still looked sad.

"Let's go to the sitting room so we'll be more comfortable," Ireland suggested. "Would you like coffee?"

"No, thank you. No more caffeine for me."

What Ireland referred to as the sitting room was actually the conference room. They had deliberately chosen an antique dining suite to serve as their conference table for contracts and paperwork. For more informal discussions and plotting a course of action, seating was arranged like a living room, with a sofa and comfortable arm chairs. The room was done in a soothing palette of browns and blues. Creating a homey atmosphere put their clients at ease and helped forge a positive relationship.

Ireland took it upon herself to bring them all a glass of water before taking her seat among them.

"What brings you here today, Mr. Dudley?" Willow asked.

"Lawrence," he reminded her. "And I'm here because I recently lost my father." All three women murmured their condolences before he continued, "The local law enforcement ruled his death as natural causes, but I know that's not the case."

"It's not?" Ireland asked.

"No. My father was perfectly healthy. He had a complete check-up just a few weeks before, and there were no issues whatsoever. I talked to him three days before he died. He said he felt fine. Then, five days ago, he died of what they insist was a heart attack."

"Have you spoken to his doctor?" Everleigh asked.

"Yes. He was as shocked as I was."

"You say 'they,'" Ireland noticed. "Who would that be? The medical examiner?"

"No. Dad lived in Lime Creek, not far across the Missouri border. It's in a rural county with little resources. As a doctor himself, my father acted as the medical examiner. Without him, the police department made a judgment call based on the absence of a visible wound."

"But you think there's something more to it than that?" Willow made a reasonable assumption based on his presence today.

"I do. My father insisted he was feeling great on Sunday. He was in good spirits, actually, but he acted a little... strange."

"Often, people don't recognize the subtle signs of an impending heart attack," Ireland said in a gentle voice. She spoke from experience. Willow's father had died of a sudden heart attack. "In hindsight, however, the clues are more obvious."

"I understand, but that's not the case. He seemed almost... happy-go-lucky. Like he was on top of the world, with nothing to lose. It was a bit out of character for him, so when I pressed him on the matter, he admitted there was a reason for his cavalier attitude." Lawrence Dudley's eyes darted toward the door.

"Did he say what it was?"

"Yes. He wasn't at all worried about his health." After an intake of air, he added, "It was his life he was worried about."

Everleigh cocked her head to one side. "Isn't that the same thing?"

"No." He looked toward the door again. Was he worried someone would overhear their conversation?

"We'll hear the front door if it opens," Willow assured him. "But I'll close the office door if it makes you more comfortable."

When she made a move to stand, he motioned her back down. With another deep intake of breath, he continued, "He was worried about his life because—because he said someone was going to kill him."

"Kill him?" Ireland squeaked. She reached for the pearls encircling her neck, a nervous habit she had when she was surprised or worried. "That's a matter for the police. Surely, once you told them that, they took his sudden death more seriously."

"I didn't tell them."

"You didn't? Whyever not?"

Lawrence looked uncomfortable. "Because... well, because he came by the information in an unconventional way."

"And what would that be?" Willow asked.

"Old Mel Helberger told him."

"Are you saying this Mr. Helberger threatened your father?"

"No, no, nothing like that."

"I'm afraid I don't understand." Willow said what they were all thinking.

"Mel is the town's oldest citizen. He has to be close to one hundred. I heard they were planning a big celebration when he turns into a centenarian. That's not what he's most famous for, however."

"That's an accomplishment within itself," Everleigh murmured.

"It is, but he's best known for his dreams. He's what some people call a—a seer." His cheeks reddened when he said the word.

"Is that right." It wasn't a question. Ireland didn't sound at all surprised

"Did your father believe that, too?" Willow wanted to know.

"No. At least, not until Mel had the dream about him. It really spooked him, you know?"

"I can see where that would make a person paranoid," Everleigh sympathized.

"That's the thing." Lawrence wore a strange

expression, as if he had just made the realization. "He didn't seem paranoid. He seemed... resigned."

"Again, he could have been feeling unwell. As a doctor, he may have recognized the signs," Willow pointed out.

"I know that's the logical assumption," Lawrence allowed. "But I don't buy it. That's why I want to hire your team."

As an empath, Everleigh's blue eyes clouded with heartbreak. The moment she had greeted him with a handshake, she experienced the grief Lawrence Dudley felt. She knew he didn't believe his father died of a heart attack and was determined to find the truth behind his death.

"You want us to prove you're right," she said. It wasn't a question.

"Or prove me wrong. Either way, I need to know the truth." His chin jutted out in a mix of defiance and determination.

"Was an autopsy performed?" Willow asked.

"Unfortunately, no. My sister and I argued about it, but she went behind my back and told the funeral home it wasn't necessary. I know autopsies can be performed after embalming, but I also know it can hinder accurate results." He blew out a weary breath and confided, "My sister is a force to reckon with. She's already pressing to read the will and hurry the probate process. I had to choose my battles."

Her mouth set in a solemn expression, Ireland once again spoke from experience. "Sisters can be... challenging."

Willow glanced at her mother; she seldom spoke about her own sister. Willow had barely known her late aunt, and her mother refused to talk about their estrangement.

Lawrence continued, "Catherine, my sister, insists we should accept things at face value and move on, but it's not so easy for me. I need closure."

"We understand that, but you're asking us to prove your father was murdered," Willow said. "Unless you offer more specifics, all we have is an old man's ominous prediction and your gut instincts. Where would we even begin?"

"I did bring this," he offered. Popping open his briefcase, he pulled out a leather-bound book. "This is my father's. The official register is at the office, but this is his personal appointment book. He made handwritten notes and observations in this one. I thought it might be of some use."

"Yes. That's a good place to start, at any rate."

Everleigh knew there was something more that he wasn't saying. "Is there something you'd like to tell us, Mr. Dudley? Anything you say will be in confidence. We're here to help you, but to do so, we need to know everything."

He fidgeted in his seat. "There is something else…"

"You can tell us," Ireland encouraged him softly.

"I want you to understand that my father was a very respected man. He was a fine doctor, an active member of his church, and served on several committees and boards. He was a pillar of the community."

When he paused for a long moment, Everleigh prompted. "But?"

"But I found some rather disturbing things when I went through his house." His words were suddenly rushed. He said them quickly, before he lost the courage.

"That's not entirely surprising," Willow assured him. "We seldom know every single aspect of another person's life."

"What I found came as a complete and baffling surprise."

The man certainly knew how to build suspense. "What was it you found?" Everleigh pushed.

"I'm not... I think..." He started and stopped twice, obviously still working it out in his head. "I think I found an illegal drug operation."

The admission stunned all three women. Of all the scenarios they had imagined, this wasn't one of them.

Willow was the first to recover and ask, "And why do you think that?"

"He had some sort of elaborate setup in his basement. A lab of some sort."

"You think he was making his own formulas and compounds for his patients?" Everleigh asked. They would need to check specific ingredients and state laws, but it wasn't uncommon for doctors to prescribe homeopathic formulas to their patients. She made a mental note to do extensive research on the matter.

His voice was low. "I don't think that was the type of drugs he was making."

Ireland delicately asked, "What kind do you think it was, dear?"

"I think he was processing weed. I found these weird drying racks. A clipboard with a very rigid schedule for production. My father was known for his note keeping. He thrived on meticulous details and checklists. I found that and more. Grinders, juicers, all sorts of gadgets. A press of some kind. Small glass bottles with droppers, jars with screw-on lids. Packaging supplies. It appeared to be a very sophisticated, full-scale operation." Lawrence dropped his head in disbelief. If he hadn't seen it with his own eyes, he would never have believed such a preposterous notion.

"I don't suppose you found a list of clients among his papers?" Willow asked hopefully.

"No. I looked. I found no mention of suppliers or customers. Wherever he kept the list—and I assure you, there was a list—he kept it carefully hidden."

"You don't think he was growing the crop himself?" Everleigh brought up the possibility.

"There's nothing to suggest that, and I have no idea when or where he could have cultivated the plants themselves. My father had a booming medical practice, a full social calendar, and now, obviously, this side venture."

Caught up in their individual thoughts, conversation stalled. After a pregnant moment, Everleigh broke the silence. "Do you think your father's death was related to his drug operation?"

Lawrence's voice sounded weary. "I don't know what to think anymore. But it certainly makes his sudden death even more suspicious, don't you think?"

Willow had to agree. "Yes, I think you're right. Mel's prophesy and your father's recent behavior are circumstantial, at best, but an illegal drug operation adds a new dynamic to the situation. With this new information, I agree there's a distinct possibility he was murdered."

"So, you'll take the case?" he asked eagerly.

"Well, I…" Caught in an uncomfortable position, Willow looked to her partners.

"You've mentioned your sister," said Ireland. "How does she feel about an investigation?"

He didn't hesitate over giving an honest answer. "She's adamantly against it. Like I said, she wants to rush probate, no doubt to get her share of his estate as soon as possible."

Everleigh picked up on what he wasn't saying. "Did she and your father have a close relationship?"

"At one time, yes. She didn't marry wisely, though, and money was always an issue. She borrowed money from our father more times than I can count, and I'm sure there were plenty of others I wasn't aware of. I do know that recently, however, he turned her down. She was quite upset. It definitely caused a rift between them."

"How recently was this request?" Willow asked.

"I don't know. I know they had a big argument just a few days ago. Definitely within the last ten days."

"Do you have a recent photo of your father?"

"Sure. I brought this file, too." He sifted through his briefcase again and withdrew a folder. "If you said yes, I wanted to have everything together for you. His birthday, photographs, details of his practice and his social life, what financial and health information I have access to, that sort of thing."

As Ireland took the folder and flipped it open, a photograph fluttered to the floor. Willow bent to retrieve it.

Her eyes landed on the face of a handsome older gentleman, and she gasped.

Her reaction didn't escape the doctor's son. "You know him? You knew my father?"

"No. No, not exactly. We, uhm, met briefly in a little diner in Gander." The simple photograph suddenly felt as if it weighed five pounds. An ominous feeling smothered the air around her. Willow's mind whirled.

The threat made by a man named Pyle. His one-hundred-thousand dollar debt. His kind blue eyes. His smooth, charming manners.

Waking in the middle of the night, knowing something wasn't right. Knowing it centered around this unknown Doc.

The missed rendezvous.

The exchange of gunfire.

"*That's* the man?" Everleigh's mouth fell open. In their collective opinion, there was no such thing as a hapless coincidence. Lawrence Dudley's presence here wasn't random. There was a reason he had chosen their team, even if he wasn't aware of it.

"Wait. What man?" Lawrence wanted to know.

Ireland had a knack for thinking on her feet. She also had the social graces to soothe over the most awkward of moments. "Willow told us about a charming gentleman she met just last week." She casually toyed with her pearls. "He advised her on having the peach cobbler, I believe it was. Or was it apple, dear?"

"You were right the first time. Peach. A very delicious peach cobbler, I might add."

Lawrence chuckled. "That would be my father. He loved his sweets."

Willow glanced at the others, knowing their

answer without having to ask. "And, yes, we'd be honored to take the case. If your father was murdered, we'd like to help bring his killer to justice."

14

"Everleigh, you go first," Ireland said. "What have you discovered about the good doctor?"

They were gathered around the conference table. Each of the partners had tackled a different facet of the late Dr. Dudley's life. After two days of individual research and digging, they came together for what Ireland called a Come to Jesus.

"Whew!" Everleigh said dramatically, dragging the back of her hand across her forehead. "I discovered his finances don't fit his persona, that's for sure. They're nothing even *close* to good."

"Do tell," her grandmother encouraged.

"What Lawrence said about his medical practice was true. He had a thriving business going. Despite that, he was in debt up to his eyeballs. And he had recently made some changes to his will and his investment portfolio, drawing a healthy chunk of change out of his family trust."

"How recently?" Willow asked.

"He called his lawyer on Saturday. Henry Piedmont, a senior partner at Walsham, Washington, Piedmont, Reese, and Yin of Springfield. After some fancy footwork on my part..." Everleigh paused to show off her emerald-green suede shoe with straps and heels, twisting it this way and that, "I spoke with Piedmont, who confirmed the rush request. The doc told him he had a dire situation come up and needed the funds immediately. Piedmont didn't say it in so many words, but he assumed it was to get his daughter out of another financial jam. The funds came out of the trust earmarked as hers."

"That's interesting," Ireland mused. "They argued, the doc supposedly refused her request for money, and then he takes it out, anyway?"

"Maybe he had enough of her mooching off him and decided it would come out of her inheritance?" Everleigh posed the question.

"That would be smart of him," Ireland agreed. "I assume she's a grown woman. Borrowing from her inheritance makes perfect sense."

"From what I have learned," said Everleigh, "she has grown children of her own. The youngest is thirty-six and still lives at home, mooching off *her.*"

"So, the doctor was footing the bill for his entire family?" Willow asked with a frown.

"Oh, Lawrence and his children are all stable, both financially and seemingly personally. Catherine's daughter appears stable enough and has a family of her own, but her sons are a different story. One, as you know, lives at home with Mommy Dearest, one is living the high life at the expense of whatever woman he is conning at the time, and one son is in prison."

Ireland's lip curled in what wasn't a smile. "Sounds like a lovely family."

"The doc had plenty of troubles of his own,

without Catherine and her leeches. Despite several large deposits into his account—yes, all cash—he was behind on all his bills. Two months ago, the power company cut off his electricity for non-payment, but he came up with enough to keep the lights on the next month. This month still looks iffy." Everleigh made a waffling motion with her hand.

Willow looked surprised. "You were able to access his bank records?"

"Dr. Dudley was old school. He kept bank ledgers at home with all the information right there at his desk. Lawrence said his father kept meticulous records. That may be so, but his records must have been written in code. I don't have a clue what these abbreviations mean." She skimmed the lines of the ledger and its neatly recorded information. "A lot of the deposits are marked *F*. One cash withdrawal is marked *B*, and another *C*."

"I wonder where A, D, and E are," Willow quipped.

"I don't know, but *G* is in here, too."

"A key would be helpful," Ireland said. "I found similar abbreviations in his appointment book, but at least there was a handy key to guide me around."

"That led you to where?" Everleigh asked.

"Like you said, a healthy medical practice. His nurse was more than happy to loan this to me. The clinic keeps electronic records, but she said Dr. Dudley insisted on keeping his own calendar with his own notes."

"She actually let you bring that home?" Not that she doubted her grandmother, but Everleigh found it hard to believe. "What about breaking privacy laws? Has she never heard of HIPPA?"

Ireland shrugged a slender shoulder. "Beats me. I put my hand on her arm, sweetly asked if I could see his appointment calendar, and she just handed it over. She didn't seem too concerned about breaking any laws."

"Landee!" Willow gasped. "I can't believe you used your gift of persuasion to trick that poor woman!"

"I didn't. Honestly. I wasn't trying to persuade her when I touched her arm; I was trying to console her. She is genuinely grieving her late boss. But I asked, and she offered. I just happened to be touching her arm at the time."

"I'm not sure I buy that," Willow said with a cautious sidelong look, "but I won't quibble over our good fortune. Did you find anything helpful in there?"

"I found that well over half his patients are female. Of those, over half are women sixty and up."

"Not too surprising, given that women are more likely to see a doctor than men do. And we do live longer than men, so yes, I can see that happening."

"Apparently, half of *those* women have neurotic tendencies. They are the ultimate hypochondriacs, sometimes seeing him more than once a week. They complain of everything from a blood blister to a major migraine. I believe in seeking medical care when appropriate, but honestly!" Ireland huffed, one hand on her hip. "Some of these women are abusing the system."

"You think he was running some sort of insurance scam?" Willow asked. That would provide yet another angle they could investigate.

"I doubt it. If they came more than twice a month, most of them paid in cash. Did you know the doctor provided some of his services pro bono? And he even made house calls." In spite of all they knew about the man, Ireland looked impressed.

"I'm not sure they were pro bono, as much as they were a bartering system of sorts," Willow told her.

"What do you mean?"

"I've been looking through his personal planner, the one he kept at home. It seems that in exchange for his professional service, the women paid him in—"

Everleigh slapped her hands against her ears. "Please don't say sexual pleasures!"

"No, of course not." Willow looked appalled at first, but the expression gave way to doubt. "Not that I get the impression he would have refused, but as far as I can tell, they repaid him with baked goods. Other food, too, but mostly desserts. The man did, indeed, have a sweet tooth."

"Hmmm. That's interesting. And he has that in his appointment book?"

"Yes, and no. Mostly they're just notes. *I treated Janet for a tooth infection, and she brought me the most delicious banana pudding.'* That sort of thing. But there was definitely a pattern to it."

"Maybe these women were just looking for an excuse to see him and to curry his favors," Ireland said.

"Curry his favors?" Everleigh hooted. "Who talks like that anymore? Don't you mean butter him up? Get on his good side? Put some jam on his biscuit? Brown nose?"

"There's no need to be vulgar, dear. I'm merely pointing out that these women apparently had feelings for Dr. Dudley and knew they had a lot of competition. They could have been looking for a way to get his attention."

"They do say the way to a man's heart is through his stomach," Willow mused.

"*They*," Everleigh retorted, "are sadly out of tune with the real world. Men can cook for themselves."

"I think we're getting a little sidetracked here." Willow called attention back to the case. "Whatever the motive, it seems many of his clients were making excuses to see him, and he encouraged it as long as they fed him sweets."

"What about the house calls?"

"He notes those in here, too. *'Bill Hettle suffered another round of gout so severe, he couldn't abide wearing shoes. I saw him at his home last evening and treated him with a strong dose of black cherry juice. I reminded him to limit intake of night shade vegetables and tomatoes. To show her appreciation, his wife insisted I take home a deliciously seasoned roasted hen.'*" Willow read from the leather-bound book. "And here's another. *'On the way back from F, I dropped by to check on Miss Gertrude. The poor dear is having heart palpitations again and fears she might miss her eighty-fifth birthday celebration. Her daughter promised to save me a generous slice of cake if I am unable to be in attendance.'*"

Everleigh listened with her mouth hung open. "Are you sure you aren't reading some other doctor's notes from the 1800s?" she asked. "That's even worse than curried favors!"

"I hear the doctor was a true gentleman who believed in good manners and proper appearances," Ireland answered.

"Then it was all smoke and mirrors, because it is in very *'poor taste'*—" she used a stuffy, pompous accent, "to not pay one's bills, dare I say."

Her mother couldn't help but laugh. "Stop being silly. Aside from having illegal drugs in his basement, owing someone named Boss one hundred thousand dollars, refusing to pay his bills, and taking advantage of the affections of good cooks all across the county, he sounds like a perfectly lovely man."

"Now who's being silly, looking all sincere and everything? Whatcha bet this Boss is a loan shark? Obviously, the bank wouldn't loan him any more money, so the doctor had to find alternative funding options."

"Like we said the first day, we were all but certain Boss, or at least his lynch man, was the one to murder Dr. Dudley," Ireland agreed. "He reneged on his loan, so he paid the price."

Willow nodded. "But then we realized the doctor was found dead at home, which explained why he missed his meeting at Murder Rocks."

"So, either Boss was impatient and killed him anyway, or he had nothing to do with his death," Everleigh added.

"And let's face it. We're still not certain he was murdered," Ireland agreed. "The stress of Old Mel's prediction, not to mention the doctor's questionable lifestyle, could have caused him to have a true heart attack."

"That's true, but I agree with Lawrence. There's more to this. Why else did I have such a strong premonition that morning? It was the very morning he died, and I knew it had something to do with him.

At the time, I didn't even know his name, just that something bad was about to happen. I'd say murder is about as bad as it gets."

"Death, itself, could qualify," Ireland protested gently.

Willow shook her head in disagreement. "The feeling was too strong. The shadows were dark, and I had trouble breathing. I knew it was something very bad, as in evil. Death is sad, but it's inevitable for us all. Murder is evil."

Ireland trusted her daughter's instincts. "So, we're going on the assumption of murder. It's unlikely one of these dessert-dealing ladies did it, so who does that leave us? And how did they make it look like a natural death?"

"I've been thinking about that," Willow said. "I don't know how closely anyone examined his body. What if his neck was broken and no one noticed? That's something evil men know how to do. Like evil men who work for loan sharks. Boss could still be responsible for this," she pointed out.

"They may not have looked for an injection sight, either. Someone could have given him a lethal overdose." Everleigh's voice was thoughtful.

"Or poisoned him."

"It sounds to me," Ireland observed, "as if an autopsy is in order."

Everleigh shook her head. "The daughter will never agree."

"This daughter has been quite adamant about the autopsy and the reading of the will," Ireland noted. "Does that strike anyone else as odd?"

"I've wondered about that," Willow admitted. "Did

she know her father was going to change his will? Does she think that by rushing it through, any changes he may have planned won't be taken into account?"

"She would be right, too. Regardless of what her father planned to do, only a notarized document is considered legal."

"The changes in the will *were* notarized," Everleigh informed them. "The lawyer was able to change the signature pages and had the entire thing notarized. The doctor insisted on it."

Willow nodded. "Which makes sense if he believed Mel's prediction."

"The new will is legal, which may come as quite a shock to his daughter."

"I'm sure that it will," Ireland murmured. Her eyes were narrowed in thought. "I wonder…"

"What do you wonder?"

"It's a terrible thing to think of someone, but what if the daughter was responsible for her father's death? He refused to give her the loan. She may have believed he was cutting her out of the will completely. If she was desperate enough, and evil enough, could she have done this?"

"Sad to say, but yes, I think so," Willow agreed with her mother.

"We may be up against Catherine on getting that autopsy," Everleigh pointed out, "but Lawrence will help however he can. He said his sister didn't know about what he found in the basement. He told her he didn't know where the key was and that they were locked out. I think we need to pay a visit to the doctor's house and see the basement for ourselves."

"I like the way you think. Willow, will you do the honors and call Lawrence?"

Madalyn Dudley met them outside the doctor's modest home in Lime Creek. Lawrence was in meetings all day, but his wife was happy to bring them her key.

"If you don't mind, I don't think I'll go in," she said nervously as she handed Ireland the key.

"We understand," Ireland replied in a kind voice.

"It—It's too soon. You know? I would expect to see him there, encouraging us to have a seat in what he called the parlor while he made tea. I normally don't care for hot tea, but he added something that made it special." Her eyes clouded, threatening to rain tears. "Just one of the many things I'll miss about him."

"Were you close to him?"

"He was a very charismatic man. Everyone loved him, including me. He'll be sorely missed in our family and in our community."

"We understand he was a prominent member of the community?" Everleigh asked.

"Oh, yes. He is—sorry, *was*—on all the major committees. He served on the city council for years. And he was one of the judges for the Spring Fling Festival." Madalyn's frown puckered at mention of the upcoming festival. "Oh, dear. They'll need someone to take his place, won't they?"

"Who organizes this committee?" Willow asked.

"It's sponsored by the Lime Creek Beautification Society. I believe Louise Gardner is chairwoman of the planning committee, and of course Gaye Nell

Maulkey is heavily involved. She's a former beauty contestant herself, you know."

They didn't know, and Madalyn didn't notice their non-response.

"It wasn't just Lime Creek that adored my father-in-law," the woman continued. "He served the entire county and beyond and was often asked to speak at various events or be grandmaster for parades. To know him was to love him."

"Including the ladies, I understand." Ireland's blue eyes twinkled.

"You know how some men just love women in general? Not so much womanizers, just men who appreciate the fairer sex? That was my father-in-law. He loved Lawrence's mother very much, and he still mourned her death. But he did enjoy the company of other women."

Ireland touched Madalyn's arm, her hand light and encouraging. "Did he have a special friend?" she asked conspiratorially.

"Too many to name, I'm afraid," Madalyn admitted. Under the older woman's gentle influence, she offered names. "Louise Gardner, Pauline Weeks, a woman from Gander who *cooked* for him several times a month," she put emphasis on the word cook, "Emmaline, Sally Helm... who knows how many others? Oh, and Hilda Dunway, I suspect. Her late husband and Doc were good friends, but he does seem to pay a lot of house calls to her."

"He seems to have gotten along quite well with the ladies. Does that include your sister-in-law? Did he and Catherine get along well?"

"Oh, no, not at all. They seemed to always be at

odds. Catherine had such a bright future ahead of her. Valedictorian of her class, honors student at Washington University, acceptance into the master's program… and then, she ups and marries a man with no ambition and no real means of support. Catherine supported them all these years, but she was laid off a few years ago and never found another job. She spends most of her time petitioning for early release—her son Ethan is in prison for smuggling drugs, which she insists is all a misunderstanding—and treating her youngest son Waylon like a china doll. She was constantly begging Doc for money. Waylon needs this, her car needs that. Hubby can't work because of his latest ailment, she can't work because she's their caretaker. It was always something. But Doc finally stood up to her and refused to give her any more money. I hear they had a big argument over the phone, and that she came to see him just a few days later. I don't know what happened because Doc died right after that, but she was pretty tight-lipped about it at the funeral. When we brought it up, she looked like she was sucking on a lemon."

Madalyn made a motion with her hand, and Landee's hand fell away. It took only moments for color to flood the woman's face.

"I—I don't know why I just told you all that. I shouldn't have."

"Oh, no, dear," Ireland assured her smoothly. "I asked. And anything you say to us is strictly confidential."

Willow nodded in agreement. "Do you share your husband's sentiments about his father?" she asked.

"Do you think his death was more than a health issue?"

Madalyn darted her eyes toward the house. Sadness filled her eyes. "I know that my father-in-law seemed to be a robust, healthy man, especially for his age. He was active and always so cheerful. Yes, he enjoyed a good meal and he adored sweets, but he showed no signs of someone with serious health issues. A massive heart attack seems unlikely, but I know it happens." She shook her head, still in shock over his sudden death. "But then, Lawrence told me about Old Mel's prediction. I know a lot of people don't believe in such, but Mel has almost a perfect track record. If he predicted someone was going to murder my father-in-law, then this was murder. Not natural causes."

Madalyn Dudley spoke matter-of-factly, confident in her answer.

"I promise you, we'll do our very best to prove that." Ireland patted her hand. It was a gesture of comfort, not influence.

"Just be wary of Catherine. If she knew you were here today, she would be furious. You'll probably want to talk with her at some point but don't expect any help from her. She's content to say it was a heart attack and move on to reading the will."

"Is she executor of the estate?" Everleigh asked.

"No, thank goodness! Lawrence is the legal executor, but that doesn't mean she won't take things upon herself to speed things along. Catherine is headstrong, overbearing, and self-centered. Watch out for her."

"Does she live here in Lime Creek?"

Madalyn imitated her sister-in-law. "Among these hicks? Absolutely not! She lives in Springfield."

Everleigh nodded. "At least if the neighbors call, she can't be here within minutes," she murmured.

"On that note, I'll let you ladies get on with your investigation. Just lock the door on your way out." Madalyn walked to the front door and unlocked it, deliberately not looking inside.

"Uhm, did Lawrence mention anything about a second key?" Willow asked.

"Yes. It's right here." She looked embarrassed. "If it's not too much trouble, can you go unlock the basement and bring these back to me? It's to the left, off the hallway in the kitchen. I'm just not ready to go in yet."

"Of course. I'll be right back."

As Willow disappeared into the house, Ireland and Everleigh chatted with the woman on the front porch, keeping the conversation light. Willow returned a few moments later and promised to lock the door behind them.

With a sad smile, Madalyn turned away from her late father-in-law's house and left.

<h1 style="text-align:center">15</h1>

"This must be the *parlor*," Everleigh said. "The doctor certainly had a Victorian vocabulary."

"Décor, too," Willow noted. It was outdated in a charming, nostalgic way.

"Isn't this where they found him?"

"From what I understand, he was on the sofa. He apparently overdid the desserts and lay down on the cushions. His receptionist found him that way. Although," she added, "he had lost the contents of his stomach."

"A trait of both heart attack *and* poisoning," Ireland murmured.

"Is the kitchen this way?" Everleigh asked, already headed to the left. Stepping into it, she curled her nose. "This could use an update, too."

"I agree. Some old-fashioned kitchens are endearing. This one just feels... old." Willow looked around, something she hadn't done earlier. "Hmm. Did you know how everything in the living room— sorry, the parlor—looked neat and tidy, but this room looks sort of disheveled?"

"Maybe it's because that's the room he died in?

Not to mention the mess he left behind?" Ireland suggested.

"Maybe," her daughter agreed. She opened the refrigerator and peered inside. "But someone took the time to clean out most of the refrigerator."

"And to wash dirty dishes, even if they did leave them here in the drying rack."

"Yet the floor is dirty, and I see shoe prints, especially there by the back door."

"Maybe Lawrence?"

"It looks too small to be a man's."

"Carolyn's then," Ireland guessed.

"Hmm." It was the only comment Willow made as she continued to walk around the room. "Someone emptied the trash, but something was thrown away after that." She bent to retrieve whatever it was. She turned it over in her hands. "It's a flyer from the annual Spring Fling."

"I guess it was a sad reminder there would be one less judge for the beauty pageant," said Everleigh.

Willow continued to study the room. "Something just feels off in here," she said. "I feel like it's trying to tell us something, but I don't know what."

"The kitchen is known as the heart of a home. It's not just about the food that comes out of it to sustain the body. A lot of living goes on in the kitchen. It's the love and the spirit that comes out of it to sustain the family," Ireland said sagely.

"I wonder what the spirit of this kitchen says about the Dudley family," Willow mused. "Particularly about the doctor."

"I wonder more about the daughter," Everleigh said. "She and Lawrence sound like polar opposites.

Even the doctor sounds like he was a charming and likable man. Catherine just sounds selfish."

"We are getting that perspective from her brother and his wife." Ireland called attention to the fact. "There can be a lot of rivalry among siblings, you know."

"Not really," Everleigh said with a grin. "We're both the only child." She pointed to her mother and herself.

"Then take my word for it. Siblings can't always be trusted." She turned her back abruptly, ignoring the question she saw in Willow's eyes. Now wasn't the time.

"So, we need to talk to the sister."

"Definitely. But right now, we're here to see the basement and find whatever else we happen to discover. You say it's through here?"

"Yes. The first door off the hall."

The back door was in a nook of its own. Too small to be a mudroom, but big enough for a wall-mounted coat rack and a small entry table. There was a woman's scarf on it. Willow pulled it to her nose for a sniff. She was good at deciphering scents, cataloging them into her memory for later reference. This one smelled faintly of moth balls and *Este Lauder* cologne.

She trailed behind the others to the door she had left ajar. Instinctively, Willow locked it behind them as they descended the stairs.

Everleigh let out a whistle of admiration. "Wow. This is quite a setup."

Willow found more switches to flip, lighting the space up like a football field.

"Just look at all that equipment," Ireland marveled.

"I have no idea what half of it is used for, but I imagine it has a hefty resale value."

"I can just see the ad now." Everleigh grinned as she panned her hand in the air. "'Starting your own illegal drug operation? Don't miss this chance to buy used and buy cheap!' Or maybe, 'Not your average Estate Sale! Check out our illegal drug lab equipment.'"

"I see Lawrence removed all the products," Willow noted as she walked around. "Hey, come check this out. This must have been where he dried the actual plants."

"He was probably buying his product straight from the grower," Everleigh surmised. "Buy it green, bring it here to dry, and over there to process."

"Not that I know much about marijuana, but it sounds logical to me."

Ireland saw something of interest on the wall. "Lawrence was right about his father being meticulous with his records. This is a schedule. I saw another clipboard over by the counter." She ran a manicured finger down the timetable. "And look. He was still turning and drying raw product as late as Sunday morning. Three days before his death."

"He either sold some of it before his death, or Lawrence had a lot to dispose of," Willow said.

"How do you even do that?"

"Take it to a drug dealer," Everleigh muttered with a smirk.

"I don't see Lawrence as the drug-peddling type," Willow remarked. "Then, again, his father didn't sound like he was, either. I guess you never can tell about people."

"How very true," Ireland said. She wandered back over to the counter where the doctor had presumably processed the raw plant. There were gadgets and appliances neatly arranged along the stainless steel surface. At another table, there were boxes and packing supplies.

There was also a desk tucked under the stairs, aglow with enough lighting to accommodate an older gentleman's eyes. Everleigh headed toward it.

To her surprise, the drawers were unlocked. With the keyed basement door, she supposed it made sense, but instinct told her there was another reason.

"Look what I just found!" Her eyes were alight with excitement.

"What is it?" Willow headed toward her. She had been wandering around, documenting their discovery on her cell phone.

"He kept a completely different ledger down here! What do you want to bet it has all his 'extracurricular' transactions in it?"

"We'll take it with us. What else is in there?"

"I see a bunch of receipts. Let's see." She pulled out the folder and sifted through the paper ribbons. "Hmm. To live and practice in Missouri, he certainly made a lot of visits to Arkansas and Oklahoma. I see gas receipts, restaurant recipes, and, oh! What do we have here?" She pulled out several receipts bound by a paper clip. Her chuckle sounded triumphant. "Oh, ho! Would you look at these? It seems our doctor may have had a gambling problem. These are all receipts to a casino in Oklahoma. I think it's one of those on a reservation near the Oklahoma/Missouri line."

"So, he lives in Missouri, does business in

Arkansas, and gambles in Missouri." Willow tried to make sense of his logic.

"You know the rather vulgar saying," Ireland pointed out, "about what you shouldn't do in your own front yard."

Everleigh 'hmphed' at her grandmother's refined ways. "I think you and Dr. Dudley would have had some interesting conversations. Both of you speak Victorian."

"Good manners aren't Victorian. They're timeless."

"Victorian, timeless, whatever." Willow waved away their interchange. "I think Landee makes a good point. The doctor had a sterling reputation around Lime Creek and the surrounding county. It makes sense that he carried out his nefarious deeds where not as many people knew him."

Everleigh had to agree. "You saw him in Gander. It's just over the border in Arkansas, so like we said the other day, convenient to get to but out of his service area. The Oklahoma border is a lot closer than the St. Louis casinos, so yeah, I can see that making sense."

Willow nodded. "Let's get a box, pack up anything that looks important, and take it with us. I can't say why, but I have a feeling we don't need to be here any longer than necessary."

"I agree. I'll get a box," Ireland offered.

"Anything else important in there?"

"Let me see."

The file drawer had folders for formulas, supplies, and processing instructions. Most had been printed off a website. "The things you can find online," she mumbled.

She opened the pencil drawer at her waist. She saw the expected pens and pencils, stapler, paper clips, and such. But it was the notepad that caught her eye.

Her gasp of surprise sucked the oxygen from the room and stalled in her lungs. Ireland hurried back with a box, and Willow looked concerned.

"What is it?" she asked, knowing it held the answer to some of their questions.

"It's a… it's a suspect list! Listen to this." She held the notepad with a trembling hand and read from it. *"Mel Helberger has predicted a dire fate for the end of my days, and I cannot ignore his heed. I have been living on the edge, conducting my life in ways I knew would lead to destruction. Mel says I will be murdered. Though the timing is uncertain, I sense the end is near. Should his prediction comes to pass, I offer these suspects for consideration.'"*

Everleigh stopped to roll her eyes. His flowery prose had an unmistakable Victorian ring.

The first suspects were a given, but as she read the list, her eyes widened with every subsequent name.

"Jethro 'Boss' Manahan
His assistant, known only to me as 'Pyle'
Waya Watie of the Cherokee Nation
Marijuana Growers, notably the Bateys and Fowlers"

She stopped reading, her jaw falling open in disbelief. Ireland drew in a sharp breath, and Willow looked dumbfounded. Collecting herself, Everleigh went back to the list.

"The next name looks hesitant. He seemed to start

and stop before he wrote *Hilda Dunway*. But it gets better. Maybe worse, depending on the way you look at it. He wrote a *C,* then marked it out. He wrote it again and put another line through it. It looks like his hand was trembling when he added the last name." Her voice dropped as she said, "Catherine."

Ireland played with her beads as she sifted through the names in her head. "How dreadful!" she murmured. "He suspected his own daughter."

"I know. It was one thing when we suspected her," Everleigh agreed, "but for her father to, as well? Can you imagine how he must have felt?" She ran her hand over the paper again, and tears sprang to her eyes. "I can feel it," she whispered. "I feel his anguish as he wrote it. I feel the heartbreak. Oh, that poor man." Tears streaked her cheeks, but she wiped them away before they reached the paper and blurred the ink.

"It must have been heartbreaking, knowing his daughter was greedy enough to kill her own father over money," Willow agreed. "But we can't lose sight of the other possibilities. The doctor was engaged in illegal activities, and that made him a target for a lot of people."

"Including one of our other clients," Ireland pointed out. "This puts us in a delicate situation. Or shall I say a dangerous situation. The Fowlers hired us, yet we have probable cause to believe they killed a man. I told you they were a dangerous lot. If they find out about this..." A tremble worked its way through her slim shoulders, and she held her pearls tight.

"We won't accuse them of anything," Willow

assured her mother. "We'll just feel them out. You can influence them to talk, I can sense if they're lying, and Everleigh can feel any guilt they feel."

"I doubt they ever feel guilty," said Everleigh. "I'm sure they justify it in their minds somehow."

"Whatever it is, you'll feel it. But theirs isn't the only name on the list. I assume the first three names are connected to his gambling addiction. Boss is obviously a loan shark. Which, by the way, was probably the cash withdrawal he noted in his journal as *B*. Pyle is Boss' muscle. Watie, I would guess, is connected to the casino, which could have been the notation of *G*. G for gambling," she reasoned. "Maybe the doctor skipped out on a losing bet, and this man plans to collect. I have no idea who the woman is, but I'm sure we will soon enough."

"That leaves Catherine."

"Who will be the easiest to check out, namely because we know who she is and where to find her," Willow said.

Everleigh cocked her head and stilled. "Did you hear that?"

"No. Why are you whispering?" Despite the question, Willow automatically lowered her own voice.

"Someone is in the house," Everleigh whispered more urgently. "I hear them moving around."

"Lawrence is at work. Madalyn is too emotional to come in. Who else has a key?"

"Catherine, I imagine. And probably the clinic, given that the receptionist found him."

"We need to turn off the lights," Ireland told them. She was already headed to the row of switches at the bottom of the steps.

Everleigh wasn't far behind her. "I'll turn off the ones up top, but it will be totally dark in here. Watch yourselves."

Everleigh shed her heels before padding quietly up the basement steps. She killed the lights, leaving them in darkness. Putting her ear to the door, she strained to hear what was happening on the other side.

She heard voices now, and they were coming closer.

"I don't know where that damned will is!" a woman's voice snarled. "We've searched everywhere! Winston, are your certain you looked in the hallway closet?"

"How many times are you going to ask me? I looked the last time we were here, and again today. No files magically appeared, Catherine," was the man's nasty reply.

"Waylon, you looked in his bedroom, right?"

"Yes, and I don't know why you sent me in there," another man whined. "It stinks like an old person."

"I checked last time. I just wanted someone to go behind me."

"Who keeps their room so neat, anyway?" the man grumbled. "His clothes and shoes were lined up with military precision. Even his drawers were organized. And the drawers *in* the drawers! It looked like he starched his boxer shorts."

The first man's voice faded into another room, but the woman's—Catherine's—was just outside the door. "See if you have any better luck with it this time."

There was no place to hide. Everleigh prayed the lock held as the door rattled and shook.

"You don't have to beat it down," the woman said sharply. "I don't want your uncle knowing we were here. I was hoping it would be unlocked this time or unstuck if that was the case. We'll have to think of something else."

"Let's try these. I found these keys in his office."

As a key ring jingled and he tried fitting the first one in the keyhole, Everleigh eased sideways down the stairs. Her heart stalled in her throat as the step beneath her creaked. When no one called out, demanding if someone was there, she dared another step, then another. She couldn't see anything, but she heard them still trying the lock.

"Everleigh?" Willow whispered as she neared the bottom.

"Yes. They're trying to open the lock. We need to hide."

"Where?" her mother hissed.

"Under the stairs."

"Landee's already there. She's putting everything she can find in the box."

A faint glow from her Ireland's cell phone guided them toward her. She was quietly adding papers to the box. She put in everything she could, not bothering to see what the papers were. Whether she saw them or found them by touch, they went in.

The rattling stopped, and still the door hadn't opened. Everleigh stepped from the alcove and listened. Nothing.

"I'll be back," she whispered to the others.

The basement had three narrow ventilation

windows along the rear outside wall. Now that their eyes had adjusted to the darkness, she could see a faint milky light coming through. The windows may have been the only thing in the room that wasn't pristine, and Everleigh suspected the grime was on the outside. Between the hint of light they provided and the occasional screen light on her phone, she found her way back to the stairs.

She reached the top just in time to hear a door slam. She waited, trying to hear something more. She released a sigh of relief when she heard a vehicle's engine start. To be on the safe side, she decided to wait a few more minutes before flipping on the lights.

She was thankful that she did. She heard a door open again, but this time it sounded like it was almost beside her. The back door, perhaps? Why would Catherine go around the house and come in from the back?

Unless, Everleigh worried, she knew someone was in the basement. When they had arrived, a plumber's van was blocking the driveway, and Madalyn was parked out on the curb. She had left a wide berth between her car and the van, but not enough for her mother's SUV to squeeze in. They had to park in front of the neighbor's, which Everleigh thought turned out to be a blessing, but maybe not. Not if Catherine had returned via the back door.

She heard something drop, a mutter of aggravation, and the door closed again. She wasn't certain if Catherine was coming or going. She turned her head in case the opposite ear might offer better hearing. Concentrating on picking up a sound, her eyes traveled randomly through the darkness in that involuntary way most people tended to do.

That's when she saw the shadow move past the tiny window. Whoever had opened the door was gone now, taking the back way around the house.

A few more minutes, and she dared to speak, even though her voice was still low. "I think we're in the clear. Watch your eyes." She flipped the switch, flooding the room with blinding light.

"Are they gone?" Willow asked in relief.

"I think so, but we need to get out of here."

The box of papers was heavy, so Willow and Ireland shared the weight as they carried it toward the stairs. Everleigh met them at the bottom, offering to carry it the rest of the way.

"Get my shoes. I've got this."

They paused again at the top of the stairs, listening for sounds of life. Confident they were in the clear, they opened the door. Ireland turned out the lights and locked the door behind them, pocketing the key.

By silent accord, they kept their voices low.

"It was Catherine," Everleigh told them.

"How can you be sure?"

"Her husband called her by name. I heard the car start, then someone came back in. They used the back door." She tilted her head backward as she carefully entered the kitchen.

"Was it her?"

"No clue. They were only here a minute before they left."

"That's odd."

"Maybe they forgot something.," Ireland suggested. "Hold on a sec." She moved in front of

Everleigh and peeked around the corner. "Coast is clear," she told them. "Let's get out of here."

Before leaving, Willow glanced over her shoulder. The scarf by the back door was gone.

16

As much as they wanted to go back to the office and dig into what they'd found in the doctor's basement, they all had plans for the evening.

Laura Beth had practice for an upcoming program at school, which meant Everleigh was on taxi duty. Ireland had committed to hosting their monthly book club and had to hurry home to finish preparations. Even Willow had plans for the evening; she was having a rare dinner out with friends.

Willow often joked that when she and Marcus split up, he got custody of most of their friends. Willow still kept in touch with a few of them, but it was awkward when someone brought up her ex and his new wife. She had a few old friends from her younger years, but most were married and preferred doing things as a couple. As the odd woman out, she found it awkward, if not downright embarrassing.

Tonight, however, she and two of her old friends were seeing a movie and going out to eat. They met in Branson at one of their favorite restaurants, a cozy Italian place tucked away from the show crowd.

"Tell us what you've been doing lately, Willow. It's been ages since we've gotten together!" Marsha Pinkerton said.

"Life is like that, isn't it? We're all so busy." Willow looked melancholy as she pulled apart a soft, yeasty breadstick. Its mouthwatering aroma floated up in a cloud of steam, instantly lifting her spirits. "I've been busy with the renovations of the building. And business has really picked up, so it seems I don't have a lot of time for myself."

"If I remember right, you've renovated that old building in downtown Border. Right?" Carrie Long had recently moved back to the area and was still catching up on all she had missed.

"It's a work in progress," she told her high school friend. "I started with the first floor so we could have our offices there. When that was done, I moved up. I have my own apartment up there, so the commute to work is just a staircase away."

"Ooh, I love a cozy loft apartment," Marsha said.

"I'd love to have you over sometime," Willow smiled. She didn't tell her friends that her apartment was the size of many homes.

"That sounds nice. I haven't been to Border in ages," Carrie said. "Remember that boy you dated from there, Marsha? What was his name?"

The women wandered down memory lane, reminiscing about their younger days. Willow had known Marsha since grade school. Carrie moved there when they were in junior high, and the three were best friends until graduation. After that, college, marriage, and babies tugged them in different directions.

Now, only a few bare threads held their friendship together.

It felt good being with friends again. Although she loved her family dearly, Willow spent almost every day with her mother and daughter. Laura Beth often spent the day or weekend with her. Willow wouldn't trade the time with any of them for the world, but sometimes, it was nice to be among friends her own age. People who didn't come with the baggage families so often carried.

The three women managed the situation well, but working with family was difficult by nature. Heated words, arguments, and differences of opinion came with deeper ramifications. Among family, there was no avoidance, no ignoring the other. No parting of ways. Sometimes, words were swallowed, feelings masked, and viewpoints blurred in order to keep peace.

Here among her friends, Willow didn't feel so stifled. She could admit that Everleigh's excessive use of coffee syrups and exotic coffee beans were taking a toll on their bottom line. Creating the drinks brought her such pleasure, Willow was loath to call her on it. But here, she could admit it drove her crazy. She could tell them how frustrating it was to have a mother who always looked as if she stepped straight from a *Today's Mature Woman* magazine. On days when they had no appointments, Willow often dressed for comfort. Far from simple sweats, but sometimes jeans or a comfy pair of pants. Next to her mother's neat, put-together look, she looked dowdy. Everleigh's fashionable shoes didn't help, either.

Marsha and Carrie understood that and shared

her sentiments.

The breadsticks kept coming, the wine flowed, and the delicious meal filled them all with a festive spirit. Someone made another toast to friendship, and they all took another sip of wine. Feeling the start of a buzz, Willow was glad the theater was within walking distance.

"Tell us, Willow, if there's a new man in your life." Marsha's eyes held a teasing light.

"Who has time for a man?" she replied flippantly.

For a fraction of a second, the image of a certain professor flashed through her mind. Dark hair worn a little too long and with just enough gray to make him even more sexy. That neatly trimmed goatee and startling blue eyes. It wasn't just his well-toned physique. His face had a strength all its own.

"You know, Jim has this friend—"

"Whoa. Wait. Stop right there. I don't do blind dates." To signify that was her final word, Willow took a forkful of lasagna and stuffed it in her mouth.

That's when she glanced up and saw a pair of blue eyes looking at her. There sat Tobias, an amused smile playing upon his lips.

Willow almost choked on her food. She grabbed the napkin to cover her cough. Her face flamed as she tried to recover from the embarrassing faux pas.

"Are you okay?" To make matters worse, Marsha thumped on her back like she was a child.

Willow waved her hand away. "I'm fine. Fine. I just took too big of a bite."

"Well, that's one way to shut me up." Her friend grinned. "So. That's a no to the blind date?"

"A giant no." Her eyes couldn't help but stray to

Tobias.

"Do you know that man?" Carrie asked.

"Wh-What man?"

"That good-looking one with the sexy goatee. He keeps looking at you."

Willow forced her eyes to look at her plate. "Actually, I do. He owns a great little antique store here in Branson. You should visit it sometime."

"Oh. So, he's married?" Marsha asked in what sounded like dismay.

"No. Widowed. It was his wife's dream to—" She followed the trajectory of her friends' eyes and saw what they were seeing.

A nice-looking woman sat across the table from Tobias. Willow had seen one of his sisters at the store. From the way this woman smiled at him, she assumed this wasn't the other one. Tobias' attention was now on the blonde and he, too, was smiling.

"Uhm, to own the store," Willow finished lamely. She cleared her throat, determined to sound more confident. She absolutely did *not* have time for a man in her life. "The name of the shop is *Years Ago Antiques and Curiosities*. And there's a little diner next to it that serves the most delicious tomato basil soup. We should make that our next outing!" She took a healthy gulp of wine.

"Really? I thought maybe..." Carrie glanced at Tobias, then back to her friend.

"You thought what? That I could get you a discount?" Willow teased. She stamped a smile on her face and forced the lilt into her voice.

Carrie played along with Willow's charade and laughed lightly. "Something like that."

Marsha was quick to change the subject. "I hope this movie is as good as the book. I hear it has great reviews."

"Yes, but by who? Unless they read the book, people won't know what they were missing." Willow was eager to take the spotlight off herself. "I don't think I've ever seen a movie that lived up to the book."

"Oh, absolutely! With a book, you get so much more depth. A movie is the condensed version, so you miss out on a lot of key details and back story," Carrie agreed.

"To books!" Willow raised her glass in another toast. With great care, she avoided looking in Tobias' direction.

The women were almost done. They had declined dessert and already thanked the server for their tickets when Willow felt Tobias approach. She was bent to retrieve her purse, but she knew he was there.

Straightening, her blue eyes met his.

"I see I'm not the only one who enjoys a good Italian meal." A smile toyed with his mouth.

"It's hard to find authentic Italian like they serve here," Willow agreed. She tried to smile, but she just wasn't feeling it. His date was nowhere to be seen, but Willow felt sure she was somewhere close.

He noticed she didn't smile, prompting him to raise an eyebrow. "I take it you're still mad at me for the other day?"

"I said thank you," she reminded him stiffly.

"As you rushed me out the door."

"With good reason," she reminded him.

He was sincere when he asked, "How is Everleigh?"

"Much better. Thank you for asking."

Tobias glanced up and saw the blonde waiting for him near the door. "I just wanted to stop by and say hello."

She didn't return in kind. "You almost missed us," she said instead. "My friends and I are headed to see a movie."

Tobias gave her friends a charming smile and a polite nod. "You ladies have a nice evening."

"You, too." Willow kept the smile plastered on her face as she turned back to her friends.

"You're holding out on us, girlfriend!" Carrie whispered. "And what happened the other day? Just how well do you know this man?"

"I told you. I know him through the antique shop."

"What did he do, sell something you had your eye on?' Marsha wanted to know. "How could you be mad at a man who looks like that?"

"Never mind about Tobias. We're going to be late for the show."

Marsha was fascinated. "Tobias?" she oohed. "What a fitting name! And don't look at me like that. Carrie and I are old married women. Let us have our fantasy, will you?"

The movie was good—not as good as the book, of course—but Willow had trouble concentrating. To take her mind off Tobias and his blond date, she thought about the latest twists in the Dudley case.

The doctor had suspected another one of their clients for his predicted murder. The problem was, she could see the Fowlers doing such a heinous deed.

If Mama Fowler and her brood thought *Intuitive Investigations* had double-crossed them, it could prove deadly.

From what little she knew about them, the Batey family was in the same class as the Fowlers. Snooping around either clan was risky at best, dangerous at worst.

Was asking about a loan shark any safer? If Boss sent his muscle to take care of Doc, he could just as easily do the same with them. Once upon a time, even hardened criminals hesitated to kill women and children. Perhaps in part to the push for equality, women were no longer immune to the same deadly fate as their counterparts.

Willow and her partners weren't familiar with the Cherokee or the woman named on the list, but if they were suspects, the doctor felt they were dangerous. He felt the same way about Catherine, regardless of her being his own daughter.

Was now the time to take their findings to the county sheriff?

Giving up so easily wasn't their style, but sometimes, there was more courage in knowing when to quit than there was in forging ahead.

The theater was crowded and noisy. At times, the musical scores reverberated throughout the theater, throbbing and fierce. The vibration was a living, viable thing, stealing breaths and leaving people on the edge of their seats.

Willow tuned it out. She listened to her inner voice, letting it fill her with the same intensity her fellow moviegoers felt. Theirs came from skillful composers and producers. It wasn't real. The intensity building inside her was.

17

"We forge ahead," Willow told them the next morning.

Ireland gave her a quizzical look. "What are you talking about, dear?"

"The case. I know it's dangerous. I know the logical thing to do is to take all this to the sheriff and let him sort through it. But we can't do that. We need to forge ahead."

"Of course we do," her mother said. The look on her face said there was never any question about it.

"I never doubted it," Everleigh agreed. "I've already started digging."

Their replies didn't surprise Willow. How could she have considered giving up? It wasn't in their genetics.

"Have you found anything?" she asked.

"Of course," she said with a toss of her curls. "Waya Watie is like a modern day, bad-ass warrior. He's fiercely protective of the Cherokee people and has taken it upon himself to guard and protect their casinos. He has a zero-tolerance policy for disrespect.

There's buzz about him being some sort of czar. He's pushed his way in, and there doesn't seem to be a way to get him out. But he's doing a good job, and he's honoring his heritage and his people, so the council leaders don't push."

"You're saying if Dr. Dudley was caught cheating, or if he didn't pay his debt, this Watie would take it as a personal insult to his People?"

"Exactly. Back in the day, he would have shot him with an arrow and taken his scalp. In modern day, he would just shoot him with a gun."

"But the doctor wasn't shot."

"Right. And there's nothing in his MO about lethal injections, poisons, breaking necks, or anything other than the old-school way of shooting his enemies through the heart."

"It doesn't let him off the hook," Ireland said with thought, "but we can probably put him on the back burner for now. What about this Hilda Dunway?"

"Classic story of a younger, attractive woman marrying someone twenty years her senior. When he died, she took full control of the business. *Dunway Logistics*. I know you've seen their trucks."

"Absolutely. They're a big operation."

"And now, the poor widow owns it all by herself. Dunway had a child from a previous marriage, but the evil step momma took it from her."

"From the way you're talking about her, I take it you're not impressed," Willow guessed.

"Not in the least. Look at her profile picture. Nothing about that plunging neckline says professional businesswoman. Maybe *show me your trailer and I'll take it for a ride*, but that's about it."

"No need to be vulgar, sweetie," Ireland reminded her.

"Sad to say, but her tactics seem to be working. Company profits have doubled since she took over. The odd thing, though, is that they haven't added all that many new associates. The workforce and payload haven't significantly changed. Neither have their rates."

"You're saying she may have added a side venture?"

"Nothing like a fresh mind to come up with fresh ideas," Willow murmured. "Think about it. She owns a trucking company. They go everywhere in the continental US. What better way to move drugs than with your own fleet of trucks?"

Everleigh wasn't so sure it was the right theory. "But is marijuana worth it? More and more states are making it legal. Meth and hard-core drugs bring in the big bucks. Weed is chump change."

"Business 101. The money is in the smalls," Ireland said sagely. "Look at us. How many truly big accounts have we ever had? Not many. It's the smaller cases that pay our bills. The big wigs go to the fancy, overpriced agencies. The normal people, people like you and me who need someone honest to help them, come to us."

Willow nodded in agreement. "Even where pot is legal, there's a limit to how much a person can have on them. There's always a market for a cheap, easily obtainable high."

"What are we thinking, then? Trucker gal gets the doctor to supply her with weed, and she takes care of the rest?"

"It's worth looking into."

"Then why kill him?"

"That's worth looking into, too."

"Speaking of motives and MOs," Ireland said, "does this crime fit a loan shark's image? From your experience at Murder Rocks, his lackey didn't hesitate to pull a gun. Why change to something else?"

Everleigh chewed the end of her pen. "Actually, I have a better question. Why kill him the morning of the pay off? He was supposed to meet Pyle with the cash at two pm, but he died at home just a few hours before that."

"Maybe Pyle took the money from the house and killed him out of spite. He missed the deadline, so he paid the price," Ireland suggested.

"Then why did he show up at the rocks? It doesn't make sense."

"You're right," Willow agreed. "And Lawrence said there were no signs of forced entry, the basement door and home safe hadn't been tampered with, and his father was still in his pajamas. Even if Pyle knocked, I doubt someone as fastidious as the doctor would greet guests that early in the morning."

"Okay, so Boss and Pyle go to the back of the list, along with Watie. For now, that saves us a road trip to Oklahoma," Everleigh reasoned, "but it still leaves the two most notoriously vindictive drug growers in the state of Arkansas. The Bateys and the Fowlers."

"And the two women. Don't forget Hilda and Catherine."

"I heard Catherine through the door yesterday. Like her brother said, she's definitely a force to reckon with."

"But is she capable of killing her own father?" Ireland looked doubtful.

"She was looking for the will. Lawrence says she's pushing to have it read. She probably wants to know if Daddy made good on his threat and had time to change the terms. If the doctor listed her as a suspect, I say there's a good possibility she could have done it."

Ireland shivered and summed up her distaste in one word. "Dreadful."

"Lawrence doesn't want his sister to know about our investigation just yet. She seems the easiest to approach, but we'll have to start with one of the others. Any suggestions?" Willow asked.

"That's easy enough," her mother replied. "Hilda Dunway. I'll wager none of us are eager to approach the Bateys or the Fowlers."

"Especially the Bateys. At least we have a reason to be on Fowler land." Everleigh reminded them of the one bright spot in their investigation. If not bright, it at least offered a glimmer of something positive.

"Why don't you figure out a way to approach Hilda?" Willow suggested. "Everleigh and I have met with the Fowlers several times already. We can make up some excuse to go back and overtly ask questions about the doctor."

"We need to proceed carefully," Ireland cautioned. It was a needless reminder. They all knew what was at stake. "We're dealing with potential murderers here. The trouble is, we don't know who."

"Or how many," Everleigh added softly. "Chances are, they're all capable. They just may not have been the one to kill Dr. Dudley."

With that sobering thought, she and Willow headed to Muskrat Holler. They called ahead to avoid an unpleasant greeting.

Not that the welcome they received was friendly. Once again, Georgia Fowler appeared in the doorway when they pulled up. She watched as the women tentatively opened the car doors.

When the dogs started their cacophony of yelps, barks, and menacing growls, the frowning woman stood there and made no move to quiet them. Willow and Everleigh stood rooted in place. Neither was anxious to have her leg gnawed off.

As he crossed the yard, Joe Ray's voice was sharp. "Woman! Why you just standing there like a bump on a log? Call them dogs off and welcome our guests."

With a sullen expression, Georgia did as her husband instructed. She didn't know why he didn't do it himself. Instead, she was forced to play hostess for the fancy-speaking redhead and her mama. It didn't sit well, but she knew there would be consequences to pay if she ignored him.

"Shut up, dogs. Go back to sleepin'." Her words sounded more conversational than commanding, but the animals hushed their barking. Only one still growled as the women passed, and it sounded grumpier than it did threatening.

"You know the way," Georgia said ungraciously. She let the screen door slam behind her as she went back inside.

Assuming Mama Fowler was waiting for them in

the kitchen, Willow and Everleigh picked their way through the crowded dining room.

The biting aroma of garlic and hot peppers assaulted them as they stepped into the kitchen. Three young women, two of which couldn't have been more than seventeen, at best, prepared the evening meal. A large pot boiled on the stove, smelling of onions, chili powder, and the unmistakable scent of wild game. Without doubt, tonight's menu consisted of venison chili.

Mama Fowler and two of her sons were seated at the table. Willow knew one of them was Davis, and she thought the other was Darrel. As she and Everleigh took the empty seats on either side of the family matriarch, she thanked the older woman for seeing them on such short notice.

"Did you find somethin'?"

"Not much more than what we've already told you. We did a background check on your distribution team. No one stood out as being disloyal." She couldn't very well use the term 'trustworthy.' They knowingly delivered illegal contraband, and a few were crossing state lines to do so. They were as guilty as the family who grew the weed.

"We told you that," Darrel said. "We didn't build our empire without doin' our own background check."

Everleigh resisted the urge to look around the run-down house. Their 'empire' clearly didn't include a grand mansion.

"It never hurts to double check," Willow told him.

When Joe Ray slid into the chair beside Davis, his wife was close on his heels. She stood with a possessive hand on his shoulder and glared at Everleigh from across the table.

"We thought you might'a found somebody and set 'em straight. Our books balanced for the first time in a while," Mama Fowler told them.

Willow was surprised at the news. "They did? That's good to hear."

"Maybe you two bein' here was warning enough. You better keep comin' back," Joe Ray suggested.

Ignoring him and the daggers shooting from his wife's eyes, Everleigh turned toward the woman seated at the head of the table. "When we were here before, you said the light-colored SUV was cleared to be here. But I didn't see it on the printout you gave me."

"Musta been a mistake. But like I told you, they had reason to be here."

"I also remember you distinctly told your daughter-in-law to bring us a list of all your scheduled delivery drivers. Does that mean you have some that make unscheduled drops?"

Mama Fowler bristled. She wasn't accustomed to having someone question her actions. "Never you mind. I told you they had a right to be on the farm."

This was the tricky part. Willow knew they needed to be careful of how they broached the subject of the doctor.

"We met a man recently," Willow began, leaving out the fact that only she had met the doctor, and that it had hardly been a proper introduction, "who visited Oklahoma at least once a month."

Everleigh watched the faces of their hosts while they were staring at her mother. She saw a range of emotions, from surprised to cautious.

"Not so surprisin'," the old woman shrugged. "Not but a few hours to the state line."

"This man lived in Missouri."

"Still makes sense. It borders part of Oklahoma, same as us."

"That's true. But this man was a doctor. He had a line of products he made himself, and he sold them in his office. He probably sold them in Oklahoma, too."

"A doctor, you say?" Mama Fowler's eyes narrowed slightly, but she shrugged her shoulders nonchalantly. "Good for him. I hear even doctors have trouble making ends meet at times."

"I don't know if money was a problem for him or not." Willow sounded doubtful. "He had a very lucrative side business with his infused products."

"Infused?" Davis picked up on the word.

"Don't that mean injected?" Joe Ray asked suspiciously. "Like when we inject a turkey with flavorin' before we fry it?"

"Yes, but this wasn't flavoring," Willow assured him. "This was marijuana. From what I understand, it made his products quite popular."

"Marijuana?" Mama Fowler's bark came out sharp.

Beside Willow, Davis' hands balled into fists. "*Our marijuana?*"

Darrell pushed back from the table with such force, his chair toppled to the floor. Everleigh and Willow both jumped in surprise. "I'll kill 'im!" he vowed. "That old man's been stealin' from us!"

"Sit down, Darrell," his mother demanded.

He turned his chair upright and took a seat. "You know I'm right," he insisted. "The doc didn't come this week, and it's the one week our books balanced."

Willow exchanged a look with Everleigh. She had taken a risk bringing the subject up, but it seemed to have paid off. Until now, she hadn't put the doctor and the SUV together, but it made sense.

"Was Dr. Dudley driving the light-colored SUV that night?" she asked Claudette Fowler.

"I reckon you already know the answer to that."

Her son was still angry. He slammed his fist onto the table. "I'll rip his arms right off his body!" he declared. "Then we'll see if he can make his *infused* products."

"You can't do that," Everleigh told him.

"Says who?" he challenged. "The man's been stealing from us! No wonder our books keep comin' up short. He's keepin' some of our plants and using them himself, instead of delivering them like he should've."

"I mean you can't rip his arms off his body, because it's already six feet in the ground."

"What are you talkin' about?" Joe Ray asked sharply.

Willow answered. "She means the doctor is dead. His funeral was last Friday."

"He's dead?" Mama Fowler. From the look on her face, she hadn't known about his death. None of them had.

"I'm afraid so."

"That sorry son-of—" Darrell's angry outburst was drowned out by similar sentiments from around the table.

"I can't believe he was stealin' from us." Mama Fowler still looked stunned. "He was such a dandy, what with his flowery speech and fine clothes. I didn't think he had it in him. It takes a lot of gall to cross a Fowler."

The woman sounded proud of their reputation, reminding Willow of the fact that they weren't a family to take lightly.

"I reckon if the books stay balanced the next week or two," she told the women, "we'll be owin' you a check. I'll let you know so you can drop by to pick it up."

"There's no reason for that," Georgia said quickly. "I'll drop it in the mail to them. That will save them a trip all the way out here." She actually smiled, if the tight lift of her mouth could be called such. There was still a challenge in her eyes as she stared at Everleigh.

"That sounds even better," Everleigh assured her.

"I 'preciate the work you did here," Mama Fowler told them. "Too bad Irie didn't ever come with you, but I know she keeps her distance from these mountains."

"Maybe another time," Willow agreed, getting to her feet. "Call us if the books don't balance." She was careful not to add the customary *we enjoyed working with you* she normally issued clients. Instead, she said a brisk, "Otherwise, thank you for your business."

Beneath her breath, Georgia mumbled, "It will be the last of it, that's for sure."

Coming around the table to leave, Everleigh made a point to look Joe Ray directly in the eye. "I'd appreciate it if you called your dogs off."

Georgia sputtered and fumed, but the sound was lost to her brothers-in-law's snickers.

18

Eyeball deep in paperwork gathered from the doctor's, Willow didn't hear the door open to the office. She was in the conference room with papers scattered across the antique table and grouped into piles. Ireland devoured the doctor's appointment book with its many notations and personal observations. She occasionally jotted her own notes in the nearby spiral notebook.

Tobias' voice startled them both as he spoke from the doorway.

"Oh!" Willow dropped a piece of paper when she jumped. "You scared me!"

"I do declare," Ireland added, fingers on her pearls, "you gave us both a fright!"

"Sorry about that." His smile looked sheepish. "Everleigh told me to see myself in."

Ireland quickly recovered from her shock. "Why, of course. Do come in. Would you care for something to drink? Coffee?"

"Thanks, but I'm driving," he joked. "I was in the area and wanted to drop in for a minute. I hope I'm not bothering you."

"No, not at all! We could use a break. Willow, wasn't it nice of Tobias to drop in and say hello?" Her words sounded warm, but when she turned, the look of warning she shot to her daughter was anything but.

"Of course." Her voice was flat, much like the smile she flashed his way.

"Have a seat on the sofa," Ireland encouraged. She took off her readers, folded them into a compact size, and slipped them into their tapestry holder as she stood.

Tobias' blue eyes settled on the woman still seated at the table. "Willow? Can I have a word with you for a moment?"

While she tried coming up with a graceful way to decline, her mother happily pushed her chair in.

"Thank you for the much-needed break."' Ireland patted Tobias' arm as she passed him. "I've been needing to stretch my legs for the last half hour."

She closed the door behind her as she left.

Tobias stood somewhat awkwardly in the middle of the room, until Willow finally gave in. "Have a seat,"' she said, motioning to the chair in front of her. "Sorry for the mess. As you can see, we're in the middle of a case."

"I won't take up much of your time," he promised. He pulled the chair out and sat, but he didn't scoot forward. Instead, he stretched out his legs and regarded her with thoughtful blue eyes. Contrary to his words, he acted as if he had all the time in the world.

He didn't say anything else, creating an

uncomfortable silence between them. "Can I help you with something, Tobias?" she sighed.

"I hope so. I hope you'll tell me whatever it is that's bothering you."

She motioned to the mess on the table. "Besides a very complex investigation?"

"Yes. Besides that." He leaned forward then, his attitude less casual. "Have I done something to make you angry with me?"

"I don't know what you're talking about," she denied.

"Last week, when I went to Murders Rocks to do what I thought was helping you, you acted like it made you mad. I don't understand what I did wrong."

Willow let out the breath she hadn't known she was holding. Her eyes closed briefly. "Nothing. You didn't do anything wrong, Tobias. My mother asked for your help, and you helped. I was upset with her, and I took it out on you. I've apologized for that, but I'll do it again. I'm sorry."

"And last night?"

"What about last night?" Her voice was a bit sharper than she intended.

"You barely spoke to me. And you certainly didn't smile. I had the distinct impression you were still angry with me." He nailed her with his intense eyes. "The same impression I'm getting today."

She searched for a plausible excuse. Anything that avoided a truth she still hadn't admitted to herself, that she was possibly jealous over the unknown blonde.

"My friend was trying to fix me up on a blind date." That much was true. "I explained that I wasn't interested in a relationship right now, and I knew she would read something into it if I as much as smiled at you. And I was right. The minute you left, she gave me the third degree. I had to point out that you were there with a date to get her to lay off."

"Yeah, about that..." he said slowly.

"You don't have to explain anything to me, Tobias. Your social life is of no concern to me."

"Ouch." He rubbed at his chest as if it hurt. "That's a little harsh, don't you think?"

"Why? Because we went out for coffee?"

"No, because I thought—" Seeing her cool gaze, he grimaced slightly. "I guess I thought wrong."

"I'm glad you've found someone." Willow was pleased at how sincere she sounded.

"The thing about Cherise... It's not what you think."

"Let me guess. It's complicated."

"Very."

"Like I said, you don't owe me an explanation." She would much rather he stopped right there, without humiliating her further.

"I feel like I do. There's a lot of stuff going on right now. It's just not a good time for me to—for us to—"

Willow rolled her eyes. "Please spare me the 'it's not you, it's me' routine."

"I would never insult you like that, Willow. I hoped you would know that."

"I really know very little about you, Tobias," she said, realizing how true her words were. They had gone through a traumatic event together, but that wasn't enough to build a relationship on. She knew he was a good man, that he genuinely cared for his students, that he respected the past and his elders, and that he felt he owed it to his late wife to honor her dreams. Beyond that, she knew very little about Tobias Cameron, the man.

"And I'd like to remedy that, but the timing…"

She may not have known him well, but she knew he wasn't a man to normally sound so unsure of himself, or of what he wanted to say.

"You're right," she said, letting him off the hook. "I'm swamped right now, what with this case and all. It's very complicated, with lots of possibilities and very few answers. I don't mean to be rude, but I really do need to get back to work."

"Of course. I didn't mean to keep you." He stood quickly, his expression clipped.

"Thanks for stopping by," she said. They both knew she was only being polite.

"Of course. Feel free to do the same when you're in Branson."

Tobias saw himself to the door. Just before he opened it, he turned to say, "Good luck with the case. I hope it works out for you."

Ireland booked an appointment to speak directly with Hilda Dunway. Her receptionist told her she was lucky; the woman was normally booked solid, but a last-minute cancellation opened up the slot.

Ireland arrived early. She had never visited a trucking company before, or, as their logo claimed, *logistics specialists.* Regardless, she doubted many had offices as lush as these. She had no doubt they had seen a recent remodel. Everything was done in the latest trends and the latest color palettes. It was all lovely but perhaps lost on the primarily male workforce.

With a discreet call, the receptionist announced her arrival. Ten minutes later, she ushered Ireland down a long corridor to the corner office. According to the nameplate, it belonged to *Hilda Dunway, President and CEO.*

A beautiful woman sat behind the finely crafted mahogany desk. She stood when the door opened, but Ireland saw the slight wince of pain on her face. She quickly masked it with a smile.

"Hello. I don't believe we've had the pleasure. I'm Hilda."

Ireland wanted to dislike the woman, but she had such a pleasant smile. Despite the fancy brass nameplate, she introduced herself with no fanfare.

"Iris Gamble," the alias rolled easily from her lips. "Thank you for meeting with me on such short notice."

"Not a problem. Please, have a seat."

Her office was lavishly appointed, making the waiting room look dowdy in comparison. Ireland sank into a chair she swore was made of kid leather. It enveloped her like a hug.

"What can I do for you, Ms. Gamble?"

"Please, call me Iris. And forgive me for being presumptuous, but I suspect you suffer from sciatica. Is that right?" She used her best sweet-little-old-lady voice.

Hilda's surprise showed on her face. "How—" Her voice trailed off in confusion.

"I noticed you winced when you stood." She didn't

mention that she had also read through the doctor's notes, graciously offered to her by Raley Bumgartner. There were more notes from the desk in his secret laboratory, including the recipe for his salves and tinctures. It all made for fascinating reading. "If you don't mind a little helpful advice," she went on, "there are several natural remedies that might offer relief. Peppermint, St. John's wort, and wintergreen are all effective treatments for inflammation and discomfort." As the daughter of a self-taught mid-wife and healer, Ireland had learned of those at an early age. She was less familiar with another plant mentioned in the doctor's notes. "Stinging nettle is also effective, when made into a tincture. Soak a cotton pad with it, apply it to the area, and keep in place with gauze or a bandage. Works every time."

Intrigued, Hilda Dunway tilted her head to one side. She was well-preserved, but the accompanying sag in her skin suggested she was a few years older than Willow. "As a matter of fact, I use a salve with some of those very ingredients."

"I hope they work for you as well as they work for my patients."

"Oh? You're a doctor?"

"Not in the traditional sense. I'm an herbalist and homeopathic specialist."

"How interesting. And you sell your products to your patients?"

"Yes, and they're wildly successful. I have a dear friend to thank for his guidance in marketing my… special products." After pausing ever so slightly over the words, Ireland took a tissue from her purse. With a sniff, she dabbed at her eyes. She had made certain to wear her best jewelry today, something that hadn't gone unnoticed by the other woman. Diamonds flashed on her fingers as she daintily held the tissue to her nose. "I'm sorry," she apologized. "My friend passed away last week, and I still haven't gotten over the shock. He was such a vibrant man, and so full of life. Him dying of a heart attack is just so hard to imagine."

Hilda drew in a sharp breath. Ireland was pleased to see the questions running through her companion's mind. She had planted the seeds; it was up to Hilda to nurture them to life.

"I—I lost a dear friend to a heart attack, as well," Hilda admitted. "Just last week, as a matter of fact."

Ireland's habit of clutching her pearls was slightly exaggerated. "What a dreadful coincidence! Life does have a way of catching us unawares, does it not?"

"Indeed." Hilda was still calculating the odds in her head. Ireland heard it in her distracted murmur. *Could it be they were talking about the same man?*

"Actually, he's the reason I'm here today. I spoke with him just two days before he passed, and he was thrilled to tell me about a new business venture he was considering. He made similar products to mine. In fact, he helped me with my own recipe. He was especially helpful in obtaining one ingredient in particular for me." Ireland overtly watched for the other woman's reaction.

She wasn't disappointed. Hilda Dunway's red-tinted lips parted in a gasp. Ireland knew the exact moment her heart ticked up a notch. The moment it all came together in her mind.

Ireland pretended not to notice as she carried on

with her fabricated story. "It's reached the point where my business has grown beyond my kitchen table. I'm not in the position to advertise my products, you understand, but word of mouth has made it simply explode! I spend half my time standing in line at the post office, trying to ship orders to out-of-state clients. I need a better solution, and something my friend told me sparked a similar idea for my own business. Vern didn't mention the name of the trucking firm, but before he left for Vegas, he said he had a possible deal in the making. He was considering using a commercial line to move his products. I've heard excellent things about *Dunway Logistics*, so I naturally make you my first consideration."

Hilda managed to bring her lips together, but they parted again. She was digesting everything Ireland had just told her. She finally managed a coherent thought. "Vern? As in Vern Dudley?"

"Yes! Did you know him? He was a lovely man."

"He—He's the friend I was speaking of."

"No!" Ireland looked appropriately shocked. "What a small world!"

"It certainly is. But I don't understand something. You said Vern went to Las Vegas just before he died?"

"Yes, that's right." She leaned forward conspiratorially. "He had a bit of an addiction, you know. That man loved to gamble, almost as much as he loved his desserts."

"I—I had no idea he went out of town," Hilda murmured. She still frowned, her mind busy replaying Ireland's words. "You said he had a *possible* deal in the works?"

"Yes, that's what he said. He said it had great potential. He was leaning toward moving forward with the venture, but he said he wanted to check other options first."

"He *what*?" Hilda slammed her palms down on her desk, her face filled with rage. "Why, that—" Words seemed to fail her. Fuming, she mumbled beneath her breath, "If he hadn't died of a heart attack, I could strangle him, myself!"

Ireland pretended not to hear the unguarded admission.

"Oh, dear," she said worriedly. "I can see how upset you are about his passing. Vern must have been a dear friend to you, as he was to me. Perhaps I should go. We can pick up this conversation later, once we've both had time to grieve our sudden loss."

Hilda looked at her absently, as if she had forgotten she was in the room. "Yes, yes," she agreed hastily. "That might be best."

"Please, don't get up," Ireland said, even though the other woman made no attempt at a proper goodbye. "I can see myself out. Do take care of yourself, dear. You might use some of Vern's salve on your back and try to relax."

"I couldn't rest right now if I wanted to!" she huffed. She was talking to herself again. "I can't believe he went to Las Vegas. And with *my* money, no doubt!"

"It was a pleasure meeting you, Hilda. I'm so sorry to have upset you but do take care of yourself."

Ireland saw her way out and hurried to her car. She placed a call to Willow, who put her on speakerphone so that Everleigh could hear, too.

"I think we can safely mark Hilda Dunway off our list," she said. "She was shocked to know that Dr. Dudley had gone gambling. I may have mentioned Vegas, and something about him using an alternate trucking company for his new venture. She was livid. She said—and I quote— *'If he hadn't died of a heart attack, I could strangle him, myself!'* I have no doubt she was sincere. That woman did not kill the doctor. She was furious that he had gone to Vegas with what she called *her* money."

"Well, another one down," Everleigh sighed. "That still leaves two suspects we need to check out. Catherine," Willow said, her voice dropping to add, "and the Bateys."

19

"Are you sure you want to do this?" Ireland asked her granddaughter the next day.

"Positive. And it makes the most sense." Everleigh twirled in her very short red plaid skirt. "I have the perfect in."

"But what you're doing is dangerous," Willow said.

"Hasn't everything we've done for this case been dangerous? I'll be fine, Mom. Patrick already has a connection with the Batey family."

"I'm not sure about this friend of yours, Everleigh. Isn't he the one who helped you hack into Gideon McMurray's social accounts?"

"Yes, but don't think that's his norm. He actually owns a very lucrative software company, which is why the Bateys hired him to create an accounting program for them. It gives him the perfect reason to go out there, and he'll just happen to take me along."

"Does he normally drop in on previous customers like this?" Ireland asked.

"Welll..." She drew out the word, meaning there was more to it than a routine check-up. "He may have created a tiny glitch in the system that requires his personal attention."

Willow frowned. "I thought you said this sort of thing wasn't his norm."

"It's not. Seriously."

"Why did you involve Patrick in this anyway?"

"I was having trouble finding out much about Eli Batey and his so-called farming business. I called Patrick and asked if he could help me dig in a little deeper."

"Aka, hack his accounts," her mother said wryly.

"I merely asked for help. How he went about it was none of my concern." Everleigh gave her red curls a sassy toss. "As luck would have it, they're one of his customers, giving him the perfect reason to visit the farm. It was his idea to infect one of their programs with the bug, not mine. He's already called and told them he found it when running a diagnostic checkup, so now. he'll ride in like a cowboy in a white hat, fix the problem, and be seen as a hero." She twisted her lips to one side and amended her statement. "Except he's not a cowboy, and he doesn't wear a white hat. He wears a cap, at best."

"Do you really think they're going to just open up and share all their secrets with you simply because you're a friend of Patrick's?"

"Come on, Mom, give me some credit. Of course not. Naturally, I have a plan." Her too-bright smile worried her mother even more.

"Do I even want to know what it is?"

"Probably not. Let's adopt the Don't Ask, Don't Tell policy and go from there." When her phone binged, she checked the message. "Patrick is almost here.

Promise me you won't judge him by his looks."

"Why? What does he look like?" With every revelation, this entire idea felt worse and worse.

"Remember, he spends most of his time in front of a computer. He's truly a genius, so how he dresses and how he wears his hair is the least of his concerns."

"How does he wear his hair?" Ireland asked.

"Long. Very long. As in a ponytail. I've rarely seen him in anything other than jeans and a T-shirt, and half the time, those are in sad shape. I just don't want you two to see him and freak out. Appearances can be deceiving."

"Everleigh, are you *sure* this is what you want to do?" Willow asked.

"I'm positive. Relax, will you? I've got this."

"But—"

Everleigh put one hand on her mother's shoulder, and the other on her grandmother's. "Seriously. Trust me. I've got this."

They followed her to the door, still fretting over her undisclosed plan.

"Oh, and one more thing," Everleigh said. "Patrick isn't into fashion, but he does like his cars. Some are fully pimped out, so just be warned."

"Just how rich is your friend?" Ireland asked.

"Again, I don't ask, he don't tell. I like Patrick for his brain, not his bank account." She looked out the front window. "Oh, good. He's in the Lexus, so no worries."

Waving like she was off to a grand adventure, Everleigh said, "See ya!'" and headed out the door.

"Wow. Just… wow."

Gazing through the windshield, Everleigh stared at the fancy entrance. With its thick iron rails and elaborate brick encasements, it looked as if it belonged to some magnificent country estate. It also looked impenetrable.

A large emblem in the center identified their destination as Batey Farms. That didn't keep Everleigh from an incredulous, "*This* belongs to the Bateys?"

"Yes. What did you expect?" Patrick chuckled at her expression.

"Certainly not this!"

The gates swung open as if anticipating their arrival.

"How did it do that?" Everleigh wanted to know.

"A little AI program I created for them." He said it as if it were nothing. "It recognizes vehicles and stores them into its memory. Approved vehicles have access as needed."

"And if they're not approved?"

"A guard comes down and asks you to state your business here."

"Wow." Her voice was lower and didn't sound nearly as impressed. "They must have a serious operation going on here."

"I do their computer programming. Nothing else," he reminded her. She had heard the disclaimer more than once.

"I believe you," Everleigh assured the computer guru. "Just play along with anything I might say or do."

"Am I going to like this?"

"Probably not, but it's all I could come up with."

A private blacktop road led through what Everleigh knew would be hay fields by summer. It lent legitimacy to the *Farm* claim on the gate. She wondered how far back the real cash crop grew. No doubt it was tucked deep within the boundaries of their land, away from prying eyes and interference from the authorities.

The Batey' house was nothing like the Fowlers' jumble of add-ons and afterthoughts. The two-story home was all cedar and wrought iron, with large windows and an expansive front porch. Neatly trimmed flowerbeds framed the porch, and an early spring bouquet graced a small table between two rocking chairs.

Black cameras circling the porch were unobtrusive but clearly visible.

"Nice house," Everleigh murmured.

Only two dogs came out to greet them, unlike the menacing pack at the Fowlers. She couldn't resist reaching down to pet the droopy-eared basset hound, thereby making the collie jealous. The only danger these two presented was their happily wagging tails.

When the front door opened, Everleigh braced herself for the worst. The outer facade of the Batey Farm was pleasantly impressive, but the family had a reputation for being mean.

She half-expected to be met with a shotgun, but instead, a heavy-set bearded man stepped out onto the porch. "Patrick!" he greeted with a friendly smile. "Come on in here and bring your pretty lady with you." He waved them inside enthusiastically.

Everleigh's welcome from the Bateys was the

polar opposite from the somewhat hostile greeting she and her mother had received from the Fowlers. Eli Batey had a booming laugh, and his wife Betty Lou couldn't have been more gracious. Their daughter-in-law and a granddaughter worked in the office where Patrick set up his 'diagnostic' briefcase, both of whom gave Everleigh warm smiles.

She had to keep reminding herself that these people were breaking the law. They grew illegal pot, and they put it into the hands of teenagers. Even preteens, like her own daughter. She couldn't be fooled by their hospitality.

The shiny illusion tarnished when a door slammed somewhere in the back, and voices moved their way.

"Ma! Shelby! Where's our lunch?" a man's voice bellowed.

Betty Lou consulted her watch. "I didn't realize it was already so late. The boys are here for lunch, and I don't even have it on the table! Please, won't you and Patrick stay and eat with us?"

"Thank you, but—"

"Of course you will. I insist."

In the end, they sat around the long table with the Batey family, sharing their noonday meal.

"There's more of us, but these fellas here are our sons Eddie and Hoot, our grandson Eddie Ray, and our nephew Moonshine. His real name, swear to God." Eli held his hand up in solemn promise. "Boys, say hello to our new guest."

Her welcome ranged from a polite hello, a less enthusiastic howdy, a grunt, and a silent glare.

"You get the computers back up?" Eddie Ray asked

their computer expert.

"Yeah, it should be working fine now. I don't know what made it do that." Patrick swallowed the lie with a sip of sweet tea.

"What'd you bring her for?" Hoot asked. He indicated Everleigh with a lift of his chin.

"She was visiting me, so I brought her along. That's not a problem, is it?"

A round of 'not at all' and 'of course not' echoed around the table. Three of the men, however, refused to answer. She could feel the vibes of hostility and suspicion radiating off them.

"We don't generally welcome outsiders," Eddie Ray pointed out.

"She's not an outsider," Patrick countered. "She's with me."

Moonshine agreed with his cousin. "We don't know her from a hole in the ground!"

"How do we know she ain't a snitch?" Hoot asked.

"Elijah Claude! You apologize to our guest," his mother fussed.

"No, no, there's no need," Everleigh assured him. "I don't blame your son. You can never be too careful about who you invite into your home. And you have an impressive empire here, so I understand the need for privacy."

The room grew quiet. Patrick darted Everleigh a quick look, and she saw a flash of fear in his eyes. Even if he wasn't involved, he knew more about their operation than he admitted to.

Everleigh pretended not to notice. Her heart hammered in her chest, but she sounded completely at ease. "It's cool. It's not like I'm in any position to judge you. And considering who my grandfather is, I sure can't turn you in!" She snickered at what she pretended was her own joke.

"Your grandfather?" Eli asked. His friendly voice sounded more cautious than it had before.

"You know, Vern Dudley. He was one of your distributors." She causally bit into a pickle. "Wasn't he?"

"Doc Dudley is your *grandfather*?"

"Yes, sir. He was truly a great man."

"Was?" Betty Lou asked. Her brow puckered with concern. "Did something happen to him?"

"You haven't heard?" Everleigh dropped her head, overtly watching their facial reactions. "He passed away almost two weeks ago. I already miss him terribly."

"The doctor passed away?" Eli asked in a shocked voice. It sounded genuine. "How?"

"Heart attack, they said. You didn't know?"

"No! This is the first we've heard of it," Betty Lou answered. "I'm so very sorry for you, Everleigh dear. He was such a pleasant man."

"And a good customer," Eddie agreed.

Everleigh knew to tread softly when it came to the next part. They seemed to believe her claim so far, and she was already playing with fire.

"I know things were a bit strained between you recently, but he always spoke highly of you. And he said your products were the very best."

"Strained? What are you talking about?"

She felt the tension that coiled between Hoot's shoulders. The flash of fear that struck Moonshine's heart. And the resentment that soured Eddie Jr's disposition more than it already was.

"My grandfather said… I mean, he thought…" Everleigh looked uncertain of herself. She turned her head and asked sincerely, "Weren't you unhappy with him recently?"

"I wasn't," Eli proclaimed, before looking at the others for confirmation. "Boys?"

Everleigh saw the way Hoot squirmed beneath his father's powerful gaze. "No, I reckon not."

"Don't lie to me, boys. What are you hiding?" He didn't bother looking at Eddie. He knew where he stood on the subject of the doctor.

"We ain't hidin' nothing, Uncle Eli," Moonshine said. "It's just that—" He hesitated, allowing his cousin to take over the excuses.

"We heard he was reselling our harvest, Grandpappy," Eddie Ray all but whined. "He wasn't even giving us a cut."

"Did he pay us fair and square?" Eli demanded.

The younger man dipped his head. "Yes, sir."

"For the price we asked?" he asked Hoot.

"He did."

"Then I don't understand the problem, boys. We made a business transaction and were paid a fair price. What the doc did with it after it left our hands is none of our business." His eyes bored into his nephew. "What did you do?"

"N-N-Nothing," he stammered.

Eli Batey slammed his beefy fist onto the table, rattling the dishes and silverware. "Don't lie to me, boy! What did you do?"

"Me—Me and Eddie Ray just talked to him is all. Told him we didn't like what he was doing."

"Was that your call?"

Moonshine appeared to be in his early twenties, but when he tucked his shaking hands under his legs and studied the floor, he looked a decade younger. "No, sir."

"What else did you tell him?" he asked his grandson.

"We told him to stop," Eddie Ray mumbled.

Eli shifted his gaze back to Hoot. "You knew about this?"

"Yes, sir."

"Did you put these two boys up to it?"

"I told 'em I didn't like it, is all. I told them we deserved a cut, because we did,'" he told his father defiantly. "What he did was the same as stealing from us!"

"Eddie, slap your brother," Eli directed.

Eddie looked uncomfortable, but he slapped Hoot on the backside of his head.

"You three don't have a lick of sense," Eli said in disgust. "Did you really think he was smoking all that on his own? The man was a steady customer! Of course he was reselling it. He put it in his fancy salves and tinctures. He gave me some, and let me tell you, they worked! If I find out you did something to him—"

"We didn't, Dad. I promise," Hoot replied hastily.

"We just scared him. Honest, Grandpappy."

"We were just looking out for the family business, Uncle Eli. We didn't want him cheating us out of any profits."

Eli made a growling sound deep in his throat.

"Git out of here. You three go back to work."

"But I ain't finished eating," Hoot protested.

"You are now. Git! All of you!"

The men filed out with their heads tucked low. Eddie pushed back his empty plate. "I reckon I might as well go back, too. Mama, that was a fine meal as always. Miss Everleigh, I'm awfully sorry about the Doc, and I apologize for what those three simpletons did. They had no business talking to your grandfather like that or making threats. And I'm sorry it's too late to make it up to him. He was a good man."

The sincere apology made Everleigh feel terrible. She had lied to them to coax a reaction from them. She hadn't expected sadness and true remorse, but that's exactly what she felt in the room, now that the others were gone.

They're illegal growers, Ev, she reminded herself. *Criminals. Don't go all soft on me. What they're doing is wrong. They're breaking the law. Remember that.*

Knowing it was true didn't make her feel any better.

She and Patrick left soon afterwards, but as they drove away, a little voice kept whispering in her ear. *Sometimes, even good people do bad things.*

20

The mood at *Intuitive Investigations* was glum.

"I can't believe it." Everleigh propped her arm on her desk, chin resting in her palm. "All of our best leads are evaporating."

"We haven't spoken to Catherine yet," her grandmother reminded her. "I haven't wanted to admit it, but she's probably our best lead."

"Why wouldn't you want to admit it?" Everleigh asked.

"I can't imagine a daughter killing her own father. That kind of anger and resentment is inconceivable."

"Yes, but Lawrence hired us to find the truth behind his father's death. He may not like where that leads us, but that's beyond our control," Willow said.

Everleigh suggested, "I think we should all go. Between us, we can get a better read on what she's feeling. Genuine grief. Regret. Guilt. Whatever it is, it could help us prove she did or didn't do this."

Ireland agreed. "I can bake something. It's been almost two weeks since the funeral. People have moved on with their lives and no longer bring food for a grieving family."

"Better yet," Willow said, an idea blossoming in her mind, "let's order something from the little diner where I first met the doctor. I recall he made an odd statement, something about enjoying a homecooked meal and having the cook there make meals for him. I thought it strange, because that's what eating at a little hometown diner is about. But Madalyn said a woman from Gander often came to his house to cook for him. I think that's who she was talking about. We could place a to-go order and just happen to ask a few questions while we're at it."

"Good idea. Everleigh, can you look up the number to *The Goose & Gander*?"

Her granddaughter looked up from her computer screen and smiled. "Already have. All we need to do is decide who's placing the order."

Erma couldn't have the meal ready until the next day. She was in charge of the daily specials, meaning a last-minute switch was easy. Meatloaf, the doctor's favorite, would now be offered on Wednesday. She would make an extra one to sell to them.

"You said this was Dr. Dudley's favorite meal?" Willow asked as she eyed the special order. She had come in alone, but she might need Everleigh's help to carry it all out.

"Sure is," Erma said proudly. "Meatloaf, mashed potatoes, creamed spinach, fried okra, and homemade yeast rolls. It's all there."

Willow noticed she hadn't mentioned anything sweet. From what they had been told, the doctor had an unquenchable sweet tooth.

"He didn't like dessert?" she questioned.

"He most definitely did, but this is the meal he ordered. Sometimes he ordered a pie or cobbler to take home, but mostly, he ate them here, right after his meal." She frowned suddenly, like she had tasted a green persimmon. "I don't recall a time when I delivered his meal that he didn't have plenty of pies and cakes and banana puddings already there. The last time I was there, he even had some of those fancy little bite-sized cakes with berries and real flower petals on top."

"Those sound interesting. Do you know where he bought them?"

"I don't think he bought any of it," Erma said in a snippy voice. "I think those women brought them."

It was Willow's turn to frown. "What women?"

"His lady patients, for one. But mostly those women from the Spring Fling Festival over in Lime Creek. It's a big to-do, you know. I happen to know that half of those old biddies, if not more, had their hopes pinned on Vern." She sniffed in distaste. "Made quite a spectacle of themselves. I can't tell you how many times one of them just 'happened' to stop by with a cake or a batch of freshly baked cookies for him. They ignored me like I wasn't even there!" She glossed over the fact that Vern usually failed to introduce her. When he did, he hinted that she was just his cook, and not his girl. With another sniff, she added, "And none of them were much of a cook, either! Those walnut and raisin cookies were as bitter as a hull. The honey cake was so sweet, it upset my stomach. I don't know how Vern abided them, but he said the ladies were good enough to bake for him, and the least he could do was eat the fruits of their labor." A faraway look moved into her eyes. "He was like that, you know. Talked all fancy and was polite to a fault. He couldn't hurt their feelings. He knew the next time he saw them, they would ask if he ate it, and he just couldn't lie."

Willow tried her best to keep her thoughts to herself. The man's entire life was a lie, but she wouldn't be the one to burst the cook's bubble.

"When was the last time you cooked for him?" she asked instead.

"The Thursday before his death. I usually went there a few times a month, but I didn't hear from him that week. I guess he wasn't feeling well, and now we know why."' She looked like she might cry. "Or maybe," her face hardened, "he was upset about that daughter of his! She came that night, you know, stirring up more trouble. Asking for money again."

Willow's interest spiked. "You overheard their conversation?"

Erma looked contrite. "I tried not to listen in, you know, but her voice carries."

"You said they argued?"

"I didn't say it in so many words, but yes. They did." Erma eyed the to-go bags on the counter. "She doesn't deserve this, you know. I doubt she's even grieving. All she saw in her daddy was money signs."

"How sad," Willow murmured.

It was also sad that everyone thought Catherine was capable of killing her father. The woman may not deserve Willow's pity, but the situation did. Like Ireland said, it was an inconceivable thought.

Willow thanked Erma for being so accommodating and paid for the food. Erma held the diner door open for her as she carried out the bags.

Seeing them, Everleigh jumped from the car and met her mother halfway. "Wow! How much food is this?"

"A lot! I asked her to make his favorite meal. I didn't know it would be a feast."

"She must have thought she was cooking for an army, not just three people."

"All I can say is that it'd better be worth it," Willow said. "This feast cost a small fortune. Catherine better not grumble that it's cold by the time we get there." Everleigh got into the car, placing the bag she carried on the floorboard. Willow handed her another that went on the car seat. "This is the last one," she said. "Be careful not to squash it. I think it has rolls in it."

"They smell divine." Everleigh inhaled the yeasty aroma as she got into the car. With a wiggle of her eyebrows, she grinned. "I can't promise the bag won't be a roll or two lighter when she gets it."

The woman who answered the door had a haggard expression and deep frown lines on her face. She tried to mask the lines with makeup, but the color had settled into the creases and had the opposite effect. Her hair was a brassy blond that came straight from a bottle.

"Can I help you?" she asked suspiciously, eying the three women and the white bags they carried.

"I'm Ireland Garrett. I spoke with you on the phone yesterday."

"I remember. I told you then, it wasn't necessary to come."

"Oh, but I had to, dear! "Ireland gushed. "I wanted

to pay my respects. May we come in?"

"Now's not really—"

Catherine had her hand on the door, holding it open just enough to see them clearly. Ireland caught her fingers in a gentle squeeze. "Please?" she encouraged.

Catherine stood back as they filed past her. She caught the scent of meatloaf and yeast rolls, and some of the lines eased from her face.

Noticing the way she eyed the bags, Willow held one toward her. "We know how difficult it is to think about mundane tasks like cooking when you're still grieving. We brought all your father's favorites."

The lines reappeared, but they didn't stop her from snatching the bag from Willow's hand. "I supposed you're some of *them*," she said with disdain.

"Them?" Ireland's confused expression wasn't an act.

"His fan club. His dessert pimps."

"His *what*?" Everleigh asked, uncertain she had heard correctly.

"I know all about your little ploys." She raked her eyes over Everleigh. "Although, you do look a little young for him. Most of his 'patients' are older."

"I thought he saw patients of all ages, even Ol' Mel Helberger."

"That crazy old coot who claims he can predict the future? At his age, why did he even bother with a doctor?"

"Let's go back to the 'dessert pimp' comment," Willow said. She could understand why no one liked this woman. "What does that even mean?"

"Let me carry these to the kitchen." She reached

out to take the other two bags.

Everleigh was tempted to keep them for herself, particularly the rolls. She may have accidentally squeezed the bag as she reluctantly handed them over.

While waiting, the three women took the liberty of seating themselves. They knew their unwilling hostess wouldn't encourage them to stay.

Everleigh surveyed the room. "Nicely decorated," she said from the side of her mouth.

"On Daddy's dime, I'm sure," Ireland agreed.

"When I gave her the bags, our fingers brushed. Man, does that woman have issues!"

They kept the rest of their observations to themselves. Catherine returned, dismayed to see they had made themselves comfortable.

"Back to that comment," Willow said. "I don't believe I've ever heard that expression before."

She gave a small, humorous laugh. "It's what my son Waylon calls my father's many lady friends. He lavished them with empty praise and a show of affection, and they paid him back with desserts. The entire thing was ridiculously over the top, but I never thought it would kill him!"

"Pardon me?" Ireland's eyes widened.

"From what I understand, he gorged himself on them the morning he died. The plate was right there on the table."

"You saw it?" Willow asked cleverly, hoping to trip her up.

"The sheriff told me. He said it probably contributed to my father's sudden death."

"Did he by chance mention other possible causes?"

Catherine frowned. "None at all. He said it was rather obvious. No wounds, no signs of a struggle, no indication of a fall. He said it looked like my father was reclining on the couch and suffered a massive heart attack." She spoke dispassionately.

"He didn't mention a possible injection?" Everleigh pushed.

"Injection? Like heroin? I can assure you; my father was no drug addict!" Catherine huffed.

"Actually, I was referring to poisoning."

"Poisoning? You think someone poisoned my father?"

"I simply asked if the police mentioned it."

"Of course not. Who would want to kill my father? He was maddening at times, but as harmless as a fly."

Ireland took a different tactic. She touched her hand to Catherine's knee. "We understand you had an argument with your father shortly before he passed away. That must lie heavy on your heart," she said gently.

"Where did you hear that?"

"I must confess. I make an excellent meatloaf, but I didn't prepare this meal. We bought it from a delightful little diner in Gander, Arkansas. Your father's friend Erma made it. She said it was all his favorites."

Catherine's eyes narrowed. "Is that the woman who came to the house to cook for him? It is, isn't it? And she was there! She was there the night my father and I had our last argument. She told you about it, didn't she?"

"She mentioned it, yes. She was worried you might blame yourself for what happened."

Catherine's laugh was short and bitter. "Why on earth would I blame myself? That was the last time I spoke to my father. And that night, I vowed I would never speak to him again!" She trembled with anger. "Why would I? He said some horrible things to me, and I was done."

"It's all right, dear. You can tell me. I understand why you were upset. You swallowed your pride and asked him for money, and still he denied you. That must have hurt."

Catherine was surprised to find someone on her side for once. Her brother certainly didn't understand. "Yes. Yes, it did hurt," she admitted. "I'm his only daughter. How could he just turn me away like that?"

"I'm sure you wanted to retaliate in some way. It's only natural to want to hurt him as much as he hurt you." Ireland patted her knee again. "You can talk to me, dear. You need to get it off your chest."

"I'm fine. I got my revenge," Catherine insisted coldly.

"Oh?" Ireland managed to keep her voice neutral. "What did you do?"

"I cut him off. I told him I hated him, and I hoped he got shot by a jealous husband. Or that he died from all the sweets those women brought him. I don't know how he could do that to my mother's memory. He thought I didn't know, but he flaunted them right there under my nose! I told him I'd never speak to him again. And I wouldn't have, even if he hadn't died the next week." She said the last defiantly.

Catherine folded her arms around her body, pulling away from Ireland in the process. It took a moment, but then she blinked and looked around, as if forgetting they were in the room.

"Who are you women, anyway? And why are you asking all these questions?" she asked sharply.

"You must realize how well-loved your father was," Willow said. She spoke kindly, even if she avoided a direct answer. "Not just in his community, but all over. It came as such a shock to everyone. I suppose we're all just trying to make sense of his unexpected death."

"I can't make sense of anything that's happened since my mother passed away. If she were still living, none of this would have happened." Catherine insisted. "My father would have remained a faithful husband, my mother would have been happy to loan me whatever money I needed, and my brother wouldn't be such a prick. But death comes for us all sooner or later, and I guess it was my father's time."

Catherine stood abruptly. "Thank you for the meal. I need to serve it while it's still lukewarm."

"Yes, of course," Ireland said. "Again, I'm so sorry for your loss, dear."

Everleigh thrust her hand out for a handshake. Catherine ignored the gesture, but the younger woman persisted. When Catherine relented, Everleigh murmured, "Please accept our condolences."

"You'll be in our thoughts," Willow assured her. She offered an enigmatic smile as she walked out the door.

They waited until they were on the highway before dissecting their visit.

Willow blew out a breath. "Well? What's everyone

thinking?"

"I didn't feel guilt when I shook her hand," Everleigh told them. "I'm not sure if that's a good thing or a bag thing. If she's guilty, she's more cold-hearted than we thought. And if she's not, she still has a lot of resentment and anger built up inside her. She blames her brother for her no longer being the golden child."

"I tried to get more out of her," Ireland said, "but it's possible that's all there was. I think she meant it when she said she was done with him."

"The question is why," Willow said. "Did she finally realize it was useless to beg, or was she already planning his demise?"

"Did you see shadows? Did you sense danger?" her mother asked anxiously.

"Oddly enough, no." Willow frowned. "Catherine is clearly a selfish woman. Did you notice how she said her mother would give her the money if she was still alive? All she cares about is herself. Yes, she had something to gain by her father's death, but I'm not convinced she had anything to do with it. I almost wish she were, because she's a bitter, hateful human being. But that doesn't make her a murderer."

"Looks like we're back to square one," Everleigh sighed.

"Does that mean we're going to Oklahoma?" Ireland asked.

"I'm afraid so. Either that or give up and tell Lawrence we couldn't find anything."

"Not until we've exhausted all leads," Willow predictably replied. "And actually, I have one more idea."

21

It was a beautiful day for Lime Creek's Spring Fling Festival.

Sunshine filled the sky with soft, fluffy clouds and expansive blue skies. The breeze was just enough to tease a rustle from the leaves. Laughter hung in the air. Children squealed with delight. The latest gossip passed from ear to ear. Business among the booths was brisk, and the energy of the day was high.

More than once, Dr. Dudley's name came up. Tears were hastily swept away and smiles faltered, but they remained carefully intact.

"These little petit fours are to die for!" Everleigh said with a long, lustful sigh.

"What are those little berries on top?" Laura Beth asked.

"Crystallized blueberries, frosted in sugar. Want one?" Everleigh plucked one off and offered it to her daughter.

"Mmm," Laura Beth approved.

"This really is a nice little festival," Willow said, watching the crowd milling around them. "Good traffic."

"And they couldn't ask for better weather." Ireland held her hands out as if to showcase the warm, sunny day.

"There are some interesting booths here, too. Oh, look, Sweet Pea. Isn't that the kind of drink you like? Boba tea, or something?" Willow pointed to a sign across the way.

"Yes! Mom, can I get some?" The twelve-year-old turned eagerly to her mother.

"If it's okay with your mom, I'll buy you some."

"Mom," Everleigh warned, "you're spoiling her."

"They're only young once. And don't act like your grandmother didn't spoil you, either."

"Fine, then." She pretended to sniff. "Laura Beth, you take your grandmother to browse, and I'll take mine." Everleigh looped her arm with Ireland's. "Shall we?"

They turned in opposite directions for further exploration. It wasn't a large event, but there were still a few booths and displays they hadn't yet visited.

After buying Laura Beth's tea, they wandered into a candle booth.

"This one smells good, but that one makes my nose itch." Laura Beth scrunched her face in disapproval.

"I see earrings in that booth across the way. Let's finish this row, then come back down the other side."

They made their way from one booth to the next, laughing in that way that only grandmothers and granddaughters could. They made the turn and started to pass up the first both, when something caught Willow's eye. She stopped in her tracks.

"What's wrong, Grammy? Why are you stopping?

That's just crochet stuff."

"Uhm, I want to look at the scarves."

The curl on Laura Beth's lip said she didn't understand the appeal, but she followed her grandmother inside. Willow went straight to the back wall and touched the rack of scarves.

"Can we help you with one of those, sweetie?" An older woman came up to her and smiled. "Those are made right here in Lime Creek," she announced proudly.

"Did you make these?"

"No, not that one, I don't believe. I think Tilly Orbach made that one. She's over on the next row, selling her homemade honeys, jams, and homemade candy." The woman rummaged through the rack. "I think this pink and lavender scarf is one of mine. It looks rather festive, don't you think?

"Yes, it does." Willow murmured. She wanted to know more about the scarf. It looked very much like the one she had seen at the doctor's house. The one that had disappeared after someone quickly came and went out the back door. "So, do you and your friend make all of these things?"

"Oh, no. It's a group effort. This booth belongs to the Lime Creek Ladies Club. We all made a little bit of everything."

"So, a lot of people have a scarf like this?" she asked in dismay.

"They certainly do!" the woman was pleased to say. "They've been one of our best sellers so far."

"Is this the first year you've sold them?"

"Oh, no. We sell them every year. We have medium-weight ones like this for spring and fall, lightweight ones for summer, and heavier ones for winter. Since the mornings and evenings still have a slight chill, you might want to stay in this range."

"Tell me about this club."

"Oh, are you new to the area?"

"No, but it sounds interesting. And all of you have such obvious talent!"

"Thank you. That's such a sweet thing to say. And where are my manners? I'm Emmaline Freely."

"Willow Alexander. And this is my granddaughter, Laura Beth."

"What a lovely name, and for such a lovely young lady. Tell me, Laura Beth. Do you like to read?"

"I love to!"

"Then I'd like to give you this. It's a bookmark, see? Pick your favorite design."

"Any of them?"

"Any at all," Emmaline assured her.

"I like this bluebird."

"Ah, you have excellent taste. My friend Paulette made this one."

"How much is it?" Laura Beth asked. "I have ten dollars."

"Oh, no, dear. This one is free!"

"Are you sure? Your friend might not like you giving away her bookmarks."

"Oh, you sweet angel!" Emmaline laughed. "All our proceeds go to good deeds, and I can't think of a better deed than reading."

While she asked Laura Beth about her book preferences, Willow played a conversation through her mind. Madalyn Dudley had rattled off several of her late father-in-law's lady friends. Hadn't she mentioned an Emmaline and a Paulette, along with others? That's when she told them about Hilda Dunway, and a woman from Gander, who turned out to be Erma. What were the odds of having another Emmaline and Paulette in such a small town?

Trying not to be too obvious, Willow sniffed for hints of *Este Lauder* perfume. She went so far as to nestle her face into one of the scarves.

"They're so soft, don't you think?" Emmaline smiled, mistaking her actions as interest.

"Yes. I just can't decide..." She looked indecisive.

"You could always buy more than one," Emmaline teased. "Louise, our president and the head of our planning committee for the Spring Fling Festival, made this one. Isn't it lovely?"

Louise. That was another of the names Madalyn mentioned.

Surely, this was no coincidence. Lime Creek was a small town. There couldn't be too many women with the names Louise, Emmaline, and Paulette residing there.

As Emmaline reached across her to pull out a scarf in vivid spring colors, Willow caught the distinctive scent of *Este Lauder.*

"When—When does your group meet?"

"The first Wednesday of every month." Emmaline cocked her head sideways. "Why do you ask?"

Willow was relieved to see two women step into the booth. "Uhm, you have more customers. I'll just browse here while you help them find something."

As Emmaline greeted the newcomers, Willow suggested that Laura Beth go on to the next booth and select something special to give her mother for

Mother's Day. The girl was happy to go explore on her own, but leaving, she called out, "Thank you for the bookmark!" The show of good manners warmed Willow's heart.

The same heart that now hammered with excitement. She had no idea what these ladies knew about the doctor's death, but she knew one thing for certain. The Lime Creek Ladies Club had information that could solve the mysterious death of their beloved Dr. Dudley.

When Emmaline returned, Willow asked for more information about the Ladies' Club. Without Laura Beth there to overhear her wild fabrication, Willow told the woman she thought her mother might like to start a similar group in their own town. Her mother, she claimed, was lonely now that her father was gone, and spent her time sewing, knitting, and cooking, just to fill the long, lonely days. A club such as theirs sounded perfect.

She asked when they were meeting again and, as luck would have it, they would meet on Tuesday afternoon to report on this year's festival. Emmaline assured Willow that she and her mother were welcome to attend.

Willow then subtly shifted the conversation to a different topic. She told Emmaline that everywhere she went, she heard people talking about the recent loss of one of their most revered citizens.

At the mention of the doctor, tears sprang to the older woman's eyes. "He was a truly wonderful man, and he did so much for our community," she told Willow. "Last night before our beauty pageant began, we announced that we were dedicating this year's event to Dr. Dudley. We'll place a bronze plaque here in the park to commemorate how truly special he was to all of us."

"That's a lovely gesture," Willow said. "I'm sure his family will be deeply touched."

"It's the least we can do to honor his memory."

Willow purchased a scarf, thanked Emmaline for all her help, and promised to see her on Tuesday.

And as she made her way to Laura Beth, a plan formed in her mind.

On Tuesday afternoon, the planning committee met in closed session before the general meeting started at two. Some of the younger women on the committee left, needing to return to work or to pick up their children from school. The older women—the ones Willow instinctively knew had key information for their investigation—were still there when she and the others arrived.

'The others' consisted of one lone woman who wasn't part of the Planning Committee, Willow, Ireland, Everleigh, and the two people they brought with them.

While having lunch on Monday at the *Goose and Gander Diner*, the women had convinced Erma to come with them, despite her initial protests.

"Please come. The Ladies Club doesn't know it yet," Willow had told her, "but they're in for a big surprise. Dr. Dudley's son will be there to personally thank them for being among his father's strongest supporters. They dedicated their Spring Fling to him this year, and in turn, his son wants to show his heartfelt appreciation."

"Why should I be there? I'm not even from Lime Creek," the cook protested.

Ireland gently placed her hand on the cook's arm. "He mentioned you by name, Erma, asking that you be there, too. He knew how special you were to his father, and he wants you to be part of this day."

"Me?" she asked, obviously flustered.

"That's right," Willow insisted. "He appreciates how you cooked for his father at home. He said it was a highlight of his father's schedule."

"Do say you'll come," Ireland encouraged her, gently squeezing her arm.

With tears swimming in her eyes, Erma agreed.

So now, with Erma, Lawrence Dudley, and her partners in tow, Willow stepped into the community center. The room was immediately abuzz, the hum of curiosity so loud that Willow was certain it could be heard out on the highway.

Soon enough, Louise Garner called the meeting to order.

22

Emmaline Freely nervously stood before the group and introduced Willow. She wasn't sure who these other people were, and she wondered if she had made a mistake by inviting her.

From where she sat on the front row, Tilly Orbach had the strangest feeling that these people being here had something to do with her secret. Which was silly, of course. It wasn't as if her secret was a matter of life or death, after all.

Louise took over the meeting, asking their other guests to stand and introduce themselves.

"May I say something first?" Willow butted in.

Louise's mouth puckered, but she primly said, "Very well. You have the floor."

"I have a confession to make. I must admit to coming here under false pretenses." She spoke over another buzz, this one of suspicion and hushed assumptions. They flew around the room faster than a dozen flies could ever do. "Tilly, it's true that my mother is a fine seamstress and cook, but I'm afraid I exaggerated her loneliness. The truth is, she has quite a full social calendar, as well as a busy career. The real reason we're here today is so that I can introduce a special guest to you. Ladies, please allow me to introduce Lawrence Dudley, the son of Dr. Vern Dudley. He would like to say a few words to you, if he may."

The women were so stunned, no one said a word.

Lawrence stood and gave a gracious speech befitting his father's fondness for flowery words. He used phrases from a generation long past, bringing comfort to the hurting hearts who longed to hear his father's voice again. He thanked the women for their kindness toward his father, for supplying him with the sweets and foods he so loved, and for dedicating their recent Spring Fling to his memory. Lawrence's speech brought a few chuckles and more than just a few tears. All of the women, including Erma, were quite touched when he lavished them with praise and undying gratitude.

"And now," he told the group, "I, too, have a confession to make. I came here today not just to extend my sincere appreciation for all that you've done, but to ask for your help. You see, the sheriff ruled my father's death as a heart attack, but I don't think that's true. I am convinced there's more to it than that. My father was in excellent health. He had just had a checkup with his own doctor, who assured me that his heart was strong and healthy. A sudden heart attack just doesn't make sense.

"I hired these fine ladies from *Intuitive Investigations* to help me find out how and why he died. I came here today to ask if you have any information, no matter how small, that could solve this mystery for me. Maybe someone here can tell me about my father's actions leading up to the day of his death. Maybe someone noticed that he was acting odd, or out of character. Maybe he was worried about something. If anyone knows anything, we'd like to speak with you after the meeting. Anything you tell us is confidential. If you know something, it will be held in the utmost confidence. Please. I owe it to my father to find out what actually caused his death." He started to sit, but he turned and added, "Thank you for indulging me today. And again, anything you can tell us will help."

The meeting didn't last long. Some of the women didn't know the doctor well and were more interested in hurrying out so they could call their friends. The grapevine would be busy that afternoon, tangled with speculation, suspicion, and rumors. The juiciest bit of gossip was relaying who stayed to speak with the doctor's son: Lucille Gardner, Midge McCann, Paulette Weeks, Emmaline Freely, and Tilly Orbach. Even that new woman, the one someone said worked at that diner in Gander, remained seated.

Now that the group had dwindled and the moment was before them, Lawrence was at a loss for words. He looked helplessly at the women he had hired, silently asking what came next.

Ireland stood, her voice soft and compelling when she spoke, and full of compassion.

"We realize this may be difficult for you. It's hard to recall exact conversations. To pinpoint what simple phrase seemed slightly off. What little thing triggered your inner antenna. We all have it. Some call it women's intuition. It's how we know to read between the lines. To hear the words that aren't being said. If any of this hits a chord, please come forward."

She looked over the small group. She was surprised to see the blurred lines, the words scribbled hastily in secret, making them difficult to read. She heard the hushed admissions, the clatter of what wasn't said aloud. Ireland couldn't decipher the jumble, but it was there, waiting to be untangled.

Willow was right. These ladies knew something.

She proceeded with caution. It was important not to mention their suspicions of murder. They needed these women's cooperation, not their resistance.

"While looking into Vern Dudley's last days, we discovered some—" She paused, searching for the right word before continuing, "—discrepancies. Some things that seemed out of character for the good doctor. That's what we're asking from you today. Anything that helps piece together the puzzle of your friend's latter days."

Ireland's quietly commanding voice was as powerful as if she had touched them. The gentle persuasion curled around the grieving women, making them feel safe. They all had secrets, and they longed to unload them from their souls. The guilt weighed them down, making their hearts heavy. It bore down on their minds and saddled their consciences with guilt.

"We can find a cozy corner to speak privately, and you can share whatever it is you remember," Ireland concluded. "Feel free to visit with any of us. Our goal is all the same, and that is to give his son the closure he deserves."

Louise Gardner raised her hand. Before she lost her nerve, she blurted out, "I have something I need to say to everyone. You are among my closest friends, and it's time I shared a secret with you. Vern Dudley and I were in a romantic relationship. His family didn't know" —she darted her eyes to his son— "so he wanted to keep it private until he could speak to them. I've felt so guilty hiding this from you. It feels good now, to get it out in the open. Vern and I were in love. His death has truly broken my heart."

Silence crackled in the air. All eyes were on Louise, as sharp and lethal as daggers. When no one spoke, when all they did was stare at her with judgment in their eyes, a nervous laugh escaped her. "Why aren't you saying anything? Paulette? Midge? Have you nothing to say? Do you hate me for hiding such a secret?" They were her two closest friends. The women she thought she could count on.

Tilly Orbach was the first to reply.

"Do you really think we didn't know?" Her voice was surprisingly flat. "Do you not realize all of us share the same secret? Everyone in this room was in a relationship with the doctor. He gave us all the same excuse. His daughter had been so close to his late wife, and he had to be careful when he broke the news about a new woman in his life. Or, his son was in the middle of an important business deal, and he didn't want to distract him. The timing was never right. He had a long list of excuses. Reasons why we couldn't come forward with our relationship."

When Willow suggested they meet with the club to gather information, she thought it would be along the lines of someone seeing the doctor talking to a stranger. Of overhearing a suspicious conversation. Something that led them to the real killer.

Not once has she expected *this.*

A different voice spoke, one the group didn't recognize. "She's right," Erma said from behind them. She had tucked herself on the second row, feeling like an outsider. But she fit in with their circle, better than they could ever imagine.

"I heard the same tale," she told them. "I work across the state line in *The Goose and Gander Diner.* That's where I met him. After a few weeks, he asked if I would consider cooking for him. Our relationship blossomed from there. I came to his house every other week, bringing a meal we had to eat in private. He promised that one day we could go out in public, but the timing had to be right." Her eyes moved sharply around the room. "I was married to a scoundrel once. I knew the signs of cheating. The hushed phone calls, the hurriedly straightened room, the lingering scent of a woman's perfume. Vern was cheating on me. He was cheating on all of us."

"No!" Louise cried. "That can't be right!"

"It is, Louise," Paulette told her, not unkindly. "You weren't the only one."

Everleigh put her hand over her heart. Louise Gardner's pain was real. She was in genuine distress. The news of her betrayal came as a complete shock to her. Everleigh could feel what Louise felt, and it broke her heart alongside the other woman's. She couldn't imagine being so blind.

"How could you—How could you *do* this to me?" she cried. Her eyes circled the room, seeking an answer from at least one of her friends. Friends who weren't her friends after all, so it seemed.

"It's not us you should blame," Emmaline told her. "Vern is the one who lied to you. He lied to all of us. He tried duping us all, telling each of us that *we* were the one he loved, even though we couldn't go public with the news."

"He used us, Louise. All of us. We all knew it," Paulette told her friend.

"Everyone but me," Louise said bitterly. She had always been such a staunch leader. A strong woman who wasn't afraid to take charge. She had always fancied herself above some people. How could she have been so foolish?

The thought ripped from her on an anguished wail. "How could he make such a fool of me?"

Tilly took a deep breath, squared her shoulders, and stood. It was time she came forward with her secret.

"He made fools of us all. But since this is a day of confessions, I have one of my own to make. I knew what he was doing, and I wanted to give him a dose of his own medicine. Knowing how much Vern loved his sweets, I decided the next honey cake I made for him would be extra special." She couldn't stop now. She had to admit everything. "I stirred in a bit of the mad honey I had harvested. Just enough to produce mild symptoms. A bit of arrhythmia, a touch of dizziness and nausea. Not enough to kill him, but he may have wished he was dead if he ate too much at once." Dropping her eyes, she made one final admission. "I made three cakes in all. The last one was a week before he died."

As her friend took her seat, Emmaline popped up

from hers. "I knew what Tilly had done," she blurted out. "So, I decided to do the same thing myself. A tiny pinch of foxgloves in his strawberry pies. The pies are small, so he never had much at one time. Just enough to make him sick."

Ireland subtly shook her head, muttering under her breath. "Nature's digitoxin. Slow pulse, tremors."

Tilly hadn't known of her friend's misdeeds, only Midge's. Foxglove was bitter, needing plenty of sweetener to make it palatable. No wonder Vern said Emmaline's pies were bitter!

"While we're spilling secrets," Midge whispered, "I have one, too." She cleared her throat as she stood and spoke louder. "My daughter has learned to make all those fancy pastries and sweets in culinary school. She knows what flowers are edible, so everything she makes is perfectly safe. My secret is this: when I took her petit fours to Vern, I switched out some of the crystallized blueberries for deadly nightshade berries. I rolled them in sugar, the same way she does hers, and replaced just one per cake. It wasn't enough to hurt, not really, but he may have had a few hallucinations, or a fast heart rate. Nothing deadly," Midge insisted.

Louise stared at the women in horror. "Do you know what you've all done? You killed him!" she shrieked.

It was Erma's turn to stand. "I may have helped," she bravely announced. "Just because I knew he was cheating didn't mean I liked it. Not long before he died, I served him a potato medley. I had green potatoes mixed in and seasoned them with chicory concentrate and ginseng. He ate two helpings. He didn't have time to eat his rhubarb pie, which is just as well. I had stirred in a few shredded leaves." Her voice dropped at the honest admission.

Ireland clucked her tongue. "Solanine toxins from the green potatoes, fast heartrate from ginseng, and insulin and gastric effects from concentrated chicory and rhubarb leaves. People should use their herbs and natural poisons responsibly," she mumbled.

Sitting beside her, Lawrence heard her low commentaries. His only response was a sad frown.

On the other side of Ireland, Willow and Everleigh exchanged surprised looks. This was so much bigger than they had ever suspected.

"Since we're all being honest, I have a secret, too," Paulette said as she took the floor. "When I make Vern a batch of my walnut cookies, I add a touch of bitter almonds for even more bitterness."

"Bitter almonds produce cyanide, Paulette," Lucille whispered.

"It also makes the cookies too bitter to eat more than one or two," Paulette said. "But if it makes his heartbeat faster or makes him feel anxious, it's little in comparison to the heartache he's made all of us feel." She lifted her chin in defiance. "Don't forget. We feel that way every single day, not just on occasion."

With all the admissions out in the open, with all their secrets spilled and souring before them, the room fell silent.

It was a long moment before Lawrence finally broke the silence.

"Let me get this straight." His voice was anything but level. It held a tremor, sagging beneath the weight of their admissions. "All of you made my father unknowingly ingest poisons and toxins. All in small amounts, yes, but poisons all the same."

No one argued, not even Louise. She was the only person who hadn't given the doctor poisoned food.

Yet she, too, had a secret.

Louise had been secretly giving the doctor a love potion, willing him to fall in love with her. She found the recipe online and mixed it herself. If the potion itself didn't work, she hoped its healthy portion of marijuana would get him hooked enough to keep coming back to her for more.

Lawrence passed his hand over his face and leaned back in his chair. He stared absently at the ceiling. Eventually, he leaned forward. He blew out a deep, haggard breath. Sat back once again. He shuffled this way and that, back and forth, and still he said nothing more.

The room was quiet, except for his unsettled shifting and the women's soft sobs. Reality hit them hard as they realized what they had done as a whole.

Their actions had been deliberate. They had all taken advantage of the doctor's penchant for homecooked meals and desserts. Each of them deliberately used natural ingredients known for having adversary effects. Some produced a fast heartrate; others slowed the heart down. Some resulted in gastric distress, and bowel or kidney problems. Many created erratic arrhythmias and difficulty breathing. The women were careful to use only small quantities each time. Just enough to make him ill, never enough to kill him.

Not individually.

But what had the effect been as a whole?

The agonizing silence stretched longer.

After a long while, Lawrence turned to the three women he had hired. His voice was low, and only for their ears. "You found nothing else?" he asked.

"Nothing," Ireland said.

"We can go back and talk to everyone again," Willow offered quietly.

Everleigh nodded. "We'll take a closer look into his Oklahoma connections."

"No," Lawrence said slowly. "No, I don't think that's necessary."

He turned back to observe the women of the Lime Creek Ladies Club. They were a pitiful-looking lot. They seemed to have aged a decade in the past hour, and they hadn't the years to spare. None could be younger than seventy. They were all mothers. Grandmothers. Widows, most likely, except for Erma. And for all he knew, her cheating husband could have died, saving her the trouble of a divorce.

These were good women. He wasn't sure how he knew such, but he felt it as surely as he felt his shattered heart. They had all made the mistake of loving his father. A man none of them had really known.

A month ago, he would never have believed his father was a drug dealer. A philanderer. A compulsive gambler. A man so deeply in debt, he would go to any means to dig himself out.

Vern Dudley had been a kind and genteel man. A good father, a loving husband, and a wonderful provider for his family. He had many wonderful qualities about him, but he wasn't a saint. Just because he was easy to love didn't mean he wasn't without flaws.

These women were the same. They had their good traits, and they had their flaws. They had big hearts. Hearts they had given to his undeserving father. And, yes, they had deliberately slipped toxins and poisons into his foods. But which of these ladies had actually killed him?

Was it Tilly, with her mad honey cake?

Emmaline and her dainty strawberry pies with just a pinch of foxgloves in them?

Or was it Erma and her potato medley? He still didn't know what danger green potatoes posed, or why all parts of a rhubarb plant weren't edible. But was she the reason his father died so unexpectedly?

Or maybe it had been Midge. Had it been her nightshade berries that killed his father?

Or was the real killer Paulette, with her bitter almond and walnut cookies?

If the police came, which of these ladies would be arrested?

And once the judge looked upon these old women with their trembling jaws, their stricken hearts, and their shattered souls, which would be taken before a jury?

Would a jury even convict them, sending them to prison for the few years they had left?

And what, Lawrence wondered, if these women had spared his father a far worse death? A cruel, painful death at the hands of men known to him only as Boss and Pyle? Perhaps these heartbroken women had done him a favor in the end.

It was something they would never know, but it was a thought that, oddly enough, brought him comfort.

Lawrence Dudley pulled in a deep, soul-cleansing breath. "No," he repeated quietly, "I don't believe that's necessary. I think some things are best left as they are. I appreciate all the work you've done on this case, ladies. You know where to send the bill."

Lawrence stood and started for the door. Halfway there, he turned back to the shocked faces watching him go.

"Ladies," he said, "thank you for loving my father. And no matter what secrets you shared here today, I am a man of my word. They will be held in the strictest of confidence."

With his father's flair for fashion, he bent at the waist and bid them good day.

The hushed silence enveloping them felt like one of Vern Dudley's embraces. Safe. Warm. Deserving.

He had betrayed them all, and in the end, they had betrayed him.

Tilly Orbach and her friends at the Lime Creek Ladies Club had secrets. They weren't a matter of life or death....

Or were they?

****

FROM THE AUTHOR

Thank you so much for reading my story! I hope you enjoyed it enough to share with others. An easy way to do so is to tell your friends, post about it on social media, and leave a review, no matter how brief, on Amazon, Goodreads, BookBub, and/or the platform of your choice. Honest reviews not only help readers find a book that's right for them, but they're the lifeblood of an author's success.

Reviews or not, I'm honored you chose this book, and I hope you'll be back for Book 3 in the series, *The Armoire's Secrets.*

Feel free to drop in for an e-visit at beckiwillis.ccp@gmail.com.

ABOUT THE AUTHOR

Best-selling indie and hybrid author Becki Willis loves crafting stories with believable characters in believable situations. Many of her stories stem from her own personal experiences. (No worries; she's never actually murdered anyone).

When she's not plotting danger and adventure for her imaginary friends, Becki enjoys reading, spending time with her family, unraveling a good mystery (real or imagined), dark chocolate, and a good cup of coffee. A professed history geek, Becki often weaves pieces of the past into her novels. Family is a central theme in her stories and in her life. She and her husband enjoy traveling but believe coming home to their Texas ranch is the best part of any trip.

Becki has won numerous awards—including two Killer Nashville Silver Falchion Awards, a dozen Texas Best's Awards, InD'Tale's coveted RONE, and been named Finalist for two Claymore Awards—but feels the real compliments come from her readers. Drop in for an e-visit anytime at beckiwillis.ccp@gmail.com, or www.beckiwillis.com.